THE FEAS

(WILLIAM) JOHN METCALFE was the son of William Charles Metcalfe, an author of sea stories for boys. Metcalfe graduated with a degree in philosophy from the University of London in 1913 and for the next two years, until the outbreak of the First World War, he taught in Paris. In 1914, he joined the Royal Naval Division and fought in the war but was invalided out in 1915; two years later, he enlisted again with the Royal Naval Air Service and in 1918 obtained a commission and served as an armament officer in the Royal Air Force.

After the war, Metcalfe obtained a post as an assistant master at a London school and began to write. His first book, *The Smoking Leg and Other Stories*, was published in 1925 and is highly regarded among connoisseurs of weird and supernatural tales. Another collection, also containing several horror stories, *Judas and Other Stories*, followed in 1931. Metcalfe also wrote a handful of novels in other genres.

In 1928, Metcalfe emigrated to New York and in 1930 married the American novelist Evelyn Scott, a prominent figure in the 1920s and '30s American literary scene. In 1939, he returned to military service with the British Royal Air Force and later again returned to the United States, where he taught at schools in Connecticut and New York. After the death of his wife in 1963, Metcalfe suffered a breakdown and was hospitalized; he died in 1965 after a fall.

By John Metcalfe

The Smoking Leg and Other Stories (1925)
Spring Darkness (1928; U.S. title: *Mrs. Condover*)
Arm's-Length (1930)
Judas and Other Stories (1931)
Brenner's Boy (1932)
Foster-Girl (1936)
All Friends are Strangers (1948)
The Feasting Dead (1954)
My Cousin Geoffrey (1956)

THE FEASTING DEAD

JOHN METCALFE

VALANCOURT BOOKS

The Feasting Dead by John Metcalfe
First published Sauk City, Wis.: Arkham House, 1954
First Valancourt Books edition 2014

Published by Valancourt Books, Richmond, Virginia
http://www.valancourtbooks.com

ISBN 978-1-941147-41-2 (trade paperback)
Also available as an electronic book.

All Valancourt Books publications are printed on acid free paper that meets all ANSI standards for archival quality paper.

Cover: A reproduction of the original jacket art by Frank Utpatel (1905-1980). The Publisher is grateful to Mark Terry of Facsimile Dustjackets, LLC for providing a scan of the original jacket.

Set in Dante MT 11/13.2

I

OUR boy, Denis, had at no time been very strong, and when his mother, whom he had adored, died suddenly, I fetched him from his boarding school by Edinburgh and let him stop a while at home.

Poor little fellow! I had tended previously perhaps to be a trifle stern with him, but we needed each other now, and I did all I could to make up to him for anything of harshness in the past and soften, for his tender sensibilities, the blow I myself felt so sorely.

No doubt, I had become a thoroughly 'indulgent' father, and would not, I think, have rued it but for that train of circumstances to be narrated. We were living, then, in the big pleasant old place 'Ashtoft,' near Winchester, which I had bought on my retirement from the army, and when Denis asked still to stay from school for one more term and 'keep me company' I was secretly flattered I expect as well as comforted. The milder southern air, and his daily rides over the downs, would do him good and he would take no harm from missing a few months of Greek and Algebra.

There was, that May and June, a French family – or rather, a father with his young son and daughter – spending part of the summer in the neighbourhood, and that Denis should like them and they him I found altogether fortunate. Cécile, my wife, had been half French, and when it transpired that our new acquaintances were not only residents of her native province but must actually (as we compared notes and worked it out together) be some sort of distant cousins, this chance encountering seemed more than ordinarily felicitous. Cécile had never tired of talking to Denis of Auvergne – its history, scenery, and above all its legends, some of them she admitted rather shocking – and we had frequently regretted that, as yet, he had not seen it for himself. He could, however, read and speak French very tolerably – putting me to a total shame – and now, in a variety of loyalty, I fancy, to his mother's memory, was doubly prejudiced in favour of anything or anyone of Gallic origin.

As for these Vaignons, – the father, who cultivated us with considerable assiduity, was, I believed, a landowner of consequence, with a château not far from Issoire. He was a lean, somewhat nervous yet taciturn man, with sunken cheeks and an unhappy brooding manner which I set down to his recent bereavement. The fact that he, too, had lost his wife last year was an added, if unspoken, reason for sympathy amongst us, and I was wholly glad that Denis had the orphaned Augustine and Marcel for his playmates. Truth compels me to confess that they weren't very prepossessing little scamps – being undernourished-looking, swarthy, narrow-eyed and quarrelsome! – but for Denis their society evidently had charm.

'This shall be *au revoir* and not goodbye, M. le Colonel,' said M. Vaignon upon leaving. 'For Denis, at the least. Denis shall come to see me in Auvergne, if you can spare him, in his holidays, while, to be quits, my own Marcel and Augustine might visit you.'

Here was a new idea! But, when I questioned him, Denis, it seemed, knew all about it.

'And would you care to go?' I asked, surprised.

'Oh, yes . . . I may, mayn't I?'

'We'll see . . . Yes, I daresay,' I temporized. 'Wait and we'll see.'

The notion had been rather sprung upon me, yet such holiday exchanges were constantly advertised in the press, and in the present instance there was an already-existing acquaintance between the families, to say nothing of a degree, if slender, of relationship. As for 'holidays,' – Denis had had plenty of *them*, lately, but he *would* be off to school again, nearer home, before so long. He had been falling behind, inevitably, in his studies, and now, I thought, he had a golden opportunity of picking up his French.

Next August I went over with him to Foant, saw him installed in M. Vaignon's château, where I stopped one night, and returned placidly enough to Hampshire with Marcel and Augustine the following day.

This arrangement remained in force for well over a year till Denis was thirteen, being renewed, after he had re-started his schooling, through several successive holidays, or parts of them. My boy's persistence and perseverance with the business, I must say, somewhat astonished me. What kind of fun could he have there, I wondered, that so attracted him? Marcel and Augustine, when they came to me as they usually did, could largely amuse each other, but Denis had no one of his own age to play with. Cécile had had a young nephew, Willi, her brother's child, but he had died two years ago, or else, I thought regretfully, my Denis might have looked *him* up and found him, possibly, congenial company. Now, even Willi's parents, who had lived within an easy drive of the château, had moved to Dijon, and Denis was reduced, as I have said, to M. Vaignon for the supply of entertainment. I was perplexed and, maybe, a shade jealous.

Thus far, I had had but that one glimpse of the château, since it was either M. Vaignon or his major domo Flébard who, on the next few occasions, took the children to and fro; and now, still wondering, I tried to recall the place more clearly.

The château was old, and generally in somewhat poor repair, though its interior was pleasing. Its exterior, and the immediate approaches, had been dusk-shrouded when we arrived, but before that I had had to hire a taxi, at an exorbitant fare, from the nearest station, a dozen miles away, and had had some chance of viewing the countryside between. It was austere, and grimly forbidding, with a burnt-out, cindery quality I found depressing. However, that didn't matter particularly, and our effusive welcome from M. Vaignon, coupled with repeated apologies for the breakdown of the car that should have met us, had reassured me, if I needed it. After Denis was in bed, my host and I had chatted till midnight, over some superlative brandy. There had been, from him, some laughing allusion to a 'haunted' turret room, but the story attached to it seemed confused and I could not subsequently recollect it.

'Do you still want to go to Foant *every* holiday?' I had asked Denis once. 'Why don't you give a trial to Uncle Michel and Aunt Bette instead? They'd love to have you there with them, at Dijon.'

'Oh *no* . . . I like it so at Foant, yes I *do*. . . .' A quick anxiety in his tone surprised me.

Till then, I had acquiesced in the arrangement somewhat lukewarmly, though certainly without misgiving; and even now it would be exaggeration to say I was at all uneasy. Simply, I felt that, from such slight and casual beginnings, the thing had somehow become too important or endured too long.

'But surely, you must be terribly dull there sometimes. What do you do with yourself all day?'

'Oh . . . there's a lot to do. We – ' He faltered, embarrassedly, and I experienced a faint, disquiet qualm. His delicacy had always caused his mother and myself concern, and at her death I had feared seriously the effect upon his health. But he had borne his share of grief for her manfully enough and, for a while, had seemed to benefit from exercise and a respite from lessons. At the moment, however, he was nervously flushed – maybe dreading my vetoing his further visits – and his eyes had an odd strained look, as if, the idea curiously struck me, he were carrying some sort of burden.

No more was said, at that time, on the subject, and the appearance, the next week, of escort Flébard – a decent, sober fellow who seemed propriety incarnate – temporarily allayed my doubts.

Yet after Denis was gone they naggingly revived. What *was* it, at the château, I could not stop wondering, that held this strong, continuing attraction for my boy? Without, exactly, scenting anything amiss, I recognised that here was an affair or situation which I had been to blame in not exploring thoroughly, and which, at least, would bear more careful scrutiny.

I resolved that, on Denis's next trip, if there should be one, I would again accompany him, or perhaps bring him back, myself, and possibly, in either case, remain with him at Foant for a day or so before returning.

That visit I remember very well. I remember, at its close, concluding that no, there was really nothing after all to worry about, and then, as a wave of unaccountable depression overcame me, feeling as vaguely puzzled and undecided in my mind as ever.

M. Vaignon, pressing me to stop longer than the three days I did, had been almost too attentive a host, scarcely indeed permitting me out of his sight. With his own children (of whom, next year he would see less, one being entered for a lycée at Bourges, the other for a convent school in the same town) he seemed stricter than in Hampshire, and I reflected wryly that, while it lasted, this exchange-system certainly gave him the better of the bargain, for there could be no comparison between my handsome, graceful Denis and his two 'replacements,' – queer, cryptic little monkeys that they were.

For my sojourn at the château it had turned out more convenient to choose not the beginning but the end of a stay there, by Denis, of four weeks. The hours passed, not disagreeably and till my final night quite unremarkably, in talking, eating, card-playing, sheer loafing, and a short series of amiably conducted tours of the estate. Upon these rambles Denis would go with us, not ill-pleased to assist M. Vaignon in the part of showman, and yet, I thought, a trifle distrait and subdued, his bright head glinting on before us in the sun. It was extremely sultry, the middle of August, and the scorched country frowned quivering around us through a heat-haze. Towards Foant, the turmoiled landscape was a gross tumble of smirched rocks, like something caught in the act of an explosion or – a more fanciful comparison occurred to me – as if these riven slabs, seared spires and pinnacles and blackened ingots of fused earth had been the 'men' which sportive devils had hurled down upon the gaming-table of the puys in some infernal tourney, and then left in disarray. I told myself I would be very thankful when my boy and I were home.

But what had chiefly struck me during my three days at the château was a peculiar faint change – for all his courtesy – in M. Vaignon. Once, when I referred casually to Denis's next visit, a strange hesitating and constrained look crossed his face.

'Yes,' he replied, without conviction. 'Ah well, we all grow up, and the best of things come to an end. . . .'

That night – the eve of our return to England – I was restless. My feather-bed stifled me, and I remembered that a winding stair outside my room, adjoining Denis's, led to a small garden. To snatch a breath of fresher air I began, in my dressing-gown, to descend the stairway, but stopped short at the sound of voices.

It was M. Vaignon, talking, I rather guessed, to Flébard.

'No, no,' the disturbed half-whisper reached me. 'We can't . . . I tell you, *hélas*, it has *come again*. . . .'

Hastily but softly I retreated. M. Vaignon's last words had been spoken with a curious emphasis – of fear or of a kind of despairing disgust – and for an instant I regretted not having waited for a sentence or two more. Undecidedly, I regained the landing, and saw a crack of light under Denis's door. I gently opened it and entered.

'Hello,' I said, 'so you can't get to sleep either.'

'No . . . It's so hot. . . .'

He was sitting up in bed, a candle burning in a wall-sconce beside him. In some way he seemed apprehensive and excited.

'It's not as quiet as you'd suppose, out here in the country,' I remarked, less from an interest in the fact than to conceal my own continuing agitation. 'I thought just now I could hear those old cows moving in the barn, – or it may have been the horses in the stables. . . .'

' – Or the ghost,' said Denis, 'in the tower room.'

I smiled, as I presumed he expected me to smile. 'Oh, does the ghost make noises?' I enquired, preoccupiedly, and with my mind still running upon M. Vaignon.

'Yes. . . .' Denis paused, smiling, too, then added, oracularly: 'Rinking noises. I – I make it make them.'

'"*Rinking* noises?" I came out of my brown study, startled, somehow, both by this odd description and by a peculiar intonation in his voice.

'Like roller-skating,' he explained. 'Ever so funny. We – .'

He had checked himself abruptly; though the smile lingered on his lips. It was a smile, I had the unpleasant intuition, that saw musingly beyond what *I* could see, – a smile of some superior intimacy and acquaintance, real or fancied. But I considered it wiser not, at this time, to pursue the subject. 'Good-night,' I said presently, and went back to my room.

After all this, I had reckoned gloomily on further wakefulness, yet, actually, fell very soon asleep, arousing with my spirits lightened and refreshed. If it were nothing worse, I remember thinking, than some absurd superstition that was afflicting M. Vaignon, then most of my anxiety was groundless. Merely, I was now tired of the business. Just one more visit, possibly, and then this holiday-exchange arrangement must begin to die a natural death.

However, as we were leaving, I had a mild resurgence of my previous qualms. M. Vaignon's looks were wan and the hand that shook mine trembled. Suddenly, a word to characterise his altered manner – the word I had been seeking, unsuccessfully three days – flashed disconcertingly into my brain. 'Guilty.' But how preposterous . . . ! What had he to feel *guilty* over? And yet . . . A shadow seemed to darken round me and round Denis too as we entered the car and waved our farewells through its windows.

But in the train and on the boat I managed temporarily to re-dismiss my bothersome forebodings. Perhaps M. Vaignon had privately decided that he had seen enough of us, had resolved gradually to drop us, and yet had found it hard frankly to tell us so. Well, *I* had felt for my part that the Vaignons latterly were bulking too oppressively and largely on our own Habgood horizon, and if the break did come eventually from their side rather than from mine, so much the better and the easier for me! I was in cheerful mood as we returned to 'Ashtoft.'

Two days had passed when the postman delivered to me a registered envelope, postmarked Foant. The enclosed letter from M. Vaignon read:

'Dear Colonel Habgood,

'It is with infinite distress that I am driven to inform you that it has become advisable for the hitherto so pleasant intimacy between our families to cease; nor can I, I am afraid, give any explanation of this deplorable necessity that could satisfy you. I am the victim, it appears, of a fantastic persecution or visitation with which it would not be fair that you should any longer be remotely and even unknowingly associated. This is the most that I am able to tell you in condonation of a gesture that must seem so brutal; – but, in effect, I have to draw a *cordon sanitaire* around myself, – not for my own protection but for that of those outside it! I can only hope, with my most extreme regrets that one whom I esteem so highly may accept this fact as it unfortunately stands, and grant me, henceforwards, the privilege of silence.

Yours,

V. de la F. Vaignon'

I replaced this amazing missive in its envelope. A little while ago I had been meditating just such a development, – but not in this style, no indeed! Was the man mad? Oddly, my predominant emotion was not of hurt, or any anger with him. It was, rather, of bewildered consternation, and even a sort of fear, as if, instead of ending, as it seemed, the real trouble were just beginning.

Somehow, the thing hit me in the face.

I did not immediately tell Denis of M. Vaignon's letter, and for over a week I was considerably exercised as to how I could best and most wisely do so. Finally, I let him know of it, saying that the Vaignons were going through some kind of private domestic crisis which would probably prevent his staying again at the château, for some while at least.

Admittedly, this was putting a mighty gloss on the affair, yet how else was I to phrase it? Probably, as I had surmised, M. Vaignon had been brooding this step for several months, and failed to muster courage to declare it verbally, – but now its absurd written, black and white, announcement was, in all conscience, blunt to crudity (whatever its excuses, and whatever the dickens 'persecution' and 'visitation' might be held to mean!) – and I could hardly show Denis *that*.

He received the news quietly, though I felt it a false and deceptive quiet. It must have been a serious matter to him, and, as I see it now, he was inwardly and desperately trying to measure its gravity and to decide how far this set-back might be neutralised or remedied and still accommodated to his own desires. I was extremely sorry for him, and cast about in my mind for anything that would render the blow less wounding, and leave him a little happier.

Oddly and soon enough he himself sought to help me out of this difficulty, but in a fashion I by no means relished.

'I think it'll be Raoul I'll miss most,' he said as if reflectively, yet with a certain patness that did not escape me. 'I told you about him, didn't I?'

' "Raoul"? No, you didn't.'

'*Did*n't I? Not Raoul Privache? Surely I – '

'No, you never spoke of him. Who is he?'

'Why, he was my greatest friend over there, in a way. I *must* have told you. . . . We caught moles and bats together, and went up the puy. He's – well, he's a sort of odd-job man I suppose you'd call him. He gardens, and fells trees, and looks after horses, and – Oh, *I* know!' Denis paused, as though struck by a sudden inspiration. 'He could come *here*. He could work for *you*. You need someone like that!

Oh, if we had Raoul here I wouldn't mind not going again to the château. . . .'

'Nonsense!' I answered brusquely. 'Now, *really*. . . . How many licenses d'you think I'd have to get for importing an article like *that* from France!'

What made my tone momentarily bitter had not been the bizarre character of the suggestion so much as the recognition, in my own boy, of a species of duplicity. For he had never mentioned this Raoul previously, and must have known it.

While most emphatically I wanted no more Vaignon echoes, of any sort, size or description.

Denis's brows had contracted in a kind of secret defiance.

'Oh, well,' he said glumly, 'I expect we'll see him here anyhow. . . . I expect he'll turn up, one day, just the same.'

And, the devil of it was, he did. We had finished breakfast, and I was lighting my pipe in the morning room when I heard a light tap at the window. Glancing up, I saw a man outside. He was short and rather shabby, but his face I could not then properly discern. In an instant, heart-sinkingly, I realised who it must be. The fellow was gesturing, and I, in turn, found myself echoing his signals, and pointing sidewise towards the front door, – which I opened for him.

He stood there, in the porch, and again, with vague nonplusment, I had the incidentally worried feeling that, somehow, I could not make out his features as plainly as I should. But at that moment there was a scamper of footsteps behind me, and Denis all but flung himself into the figure's arms. 'Raoul! Raoul!' he exclaimed ecstatically. 'Oh, I *knew* you'd come!'

'*Bonjour, m'sieu.*' Our visitant had put out a hand, which

I mechanically shook. The hand wore a mitten leaving only the fingers exposed, and in clasping them I experienced a strange repugnance. They were cold, and lifeless as a dummy's.

But the man could speak, it soon appeared, and volubly. Denis had led him to a back room giving on to the lawn, and there the creature began to chatter, presumably in French of sorts, though too quickly for my comprehension. Denis translated sketchily. 'Raoul,' it seemed, was offering me his services as general handyman. He had always wanted to live in England, and to have my son for his young master would be bliss indeed. His manner, as he waited while Denis was interpreting, was an odd mixture of deference and sly assurance.

'But, good heavens!' I protested. '*I* can't employ him. What about his labour-permit? He can't just plant himself on us like this and – '

The man sat there, impassive, his shadowed face averted. Denis was talking with him again, conveying, I supposed, the substance of my objections.

'He's staying here, in the village anyhow,' Denis announced, 'though it would be nicer if he could use our loft over the old coach-house while he was looking around. . . .'

'He shall *not* use our loft . . . !' I remember almost spluttering in my dumfounded indignation.

But, in the end, he did.

Whether a greater, and a prompter, firmness on my part would have prevented or, later on, ejected him I do not know. I believe now that it would not, and, in a sense, that what was had to be.

Since Cécile's death I had denied her child nothing, and if such 'pampering' were weakness it had at least been, hitherto, a natural and perhaps pardonable weakness. But my acceptance, or toleration, of this creature, this object, this ambiguous knot-in-a-board, with whom Denis's infatuation seemed quite inexplicable, was a capitulation to my boy's half tearful and half sullen importunities surpassing any previous indulgence.

Be that as it might, 'Raoul' took up his abode in the loft, and, thus confronted with the *fait accompli*, I realised gloomily that it would mean, now, a lot of unpleasantness and fuss to shift him. So, for the time being, and the time being only (as I tried to make it plain), he stayed.

There were nearly three weeks still to run of Denis's summer holidays, and he spent their waking hours, to my chagrin, almost entirely in his idol's company. I felt bewildered. Why, actually, had the man come here, and had there been a prior secret understanding between him and his admirer in the matter? Was his passport in order (though I presumed it must be, for him to have arrived at all), and what would the neighbours, and my own servants, think?

However, superficially and for a while, there was less trouble than I had anticipated. The fellow, to grant him his due, was unobtrusive to the point of self-effacement and indeed appeared anxious to keep out of people's way. He insisted on some pretence of working for me and occasionally was to be seen polishing boots and harness, clearing dead wood from the shrubbery, and the like. His meals he ate, usually, apart, fetching them from the kitchen, and consuming them in his loft. How he got on with my cook, Jenny, or with my maid Clara I was at first unable to find out. Probably they decided that the curious importation represented merely one more whim of the young master's and for the present let it go at that. As for my regular groom and gardner, Dobbs, he, as it happened, was in hospital, so his reactions were not yet available.

Just the same, the position was bizarre. Denis would shortly be returning to school, and then of course there could be no excuse for Raoul's remaining. I half thought, once or twice, and despite the 'silence' so mysteriously enjoined on me, of writing to 'sound' M. Vaignon on the subject, but, as may be imagined, I was pretty much on my dignity in that quarter, and had, besides, no right whatever to assume that *he* was implicated or involved in any way with Raoul.

I was on edge and out of sorts, living it seemed unreally in a kind of semi-dream. More and more I became sensible of this man Raoul's presence, irking me in a manner I could not describe. And one small item in particular still teased me. The fellow had been here, now, close on two weeks, and yet, for some reason, I had never formed a clear idea of his appearance. Either his features struck me differently at different times or had a queer indefiniteness that amounted, as it were, to nullity. It was not till later that I discovered that this little difficulty of his facelessness had bothered other people too.

One day, less than a week before the end of his holidays, Denis had started a slight cold. It seemed nothing much – and hadn't stopped his going out all morning, as was now his rule, with his obnoxious playmate on the down – but was enough, in view of the nearness of his return to school, to worry me. I remember telling him to take it easy indoors for the rest of the afternoon and then retiring, myself, to my study with the intention, I also recall, of settling, finally, my future course of action in this whole exasperating '*affaire Raoul.*'

But my deliberations had not got very far when they were interrupted by a visit from a Mr. Walstron, a local farmer to whom I was arranging to lease a meadow. Terms having been agreed to mutual satisfaction, the old man went on to gossip amiably of other things.

'Your boy misses his mother, sure-*ly*. Up there on the Winacre I met him this morning, looking right poorly, and chattering away like that, all to himself. . . .'

'To himself? Why, he – ' I faltered, confused and apprehensive.

'Well, – yes. . . . Talking, or it might have been singing, you know, and – funny thing – my two dogs, they – oh, you should 'a seen 'em. Such a snarling and a snapping . . . ! Never seen 'em act that way with *your* young lad bafore. . . .'

Presently Mr. Walstron wished me good-day, leaving me, certainly, with plenty to think over.

It was extremely strange. Denis, I knew, had gone out, not alone but with Raoul. And then – those dogs. . . . For, oddly, it had been with dogs that Raoul had achieved, as yet, his summit of unpopularity. My own setter, Trixie, could not abide him, shivering and growling quite dementedly whenever he was by, and evidently undecided whether to fly from or at him.

I was still trying to digest the implications of Mr. Walstron's story when the form of Raoul himself darkened the panes. Outwardly and otherwise well conducted, he had an annoying habit of coming round to the windows and tapping to attract attention. This time, perceiving I had already observed him, he did not tap but simply held up a hand. To my disgusted consternation I saw that the wrist and forearm were bloody.

Hurrying out, I examined his hurt. The flesh was badly lacerated. '*Chiens*,' I understood him to mutter. '*Chiens*. . . .'

Here was a further complication! Dog bites can be mischievous and I would not risk attempting to treat such wounds myself. So far, I had shirked bringing the man's residence to any official or even semi-official cognizance, but now, if the doctor were called, my precious piece of contraband must be declared and I foresaw all sorts of tiresome queries as to the fellow's position under the Health Insurance Act and any amount of stupid fuss. . . .

In the event, I summoned my old friend and adviser, Goderich, who had attended Cécile during her last illness. He dressed Raoul's arm and, while on the spot, looked at my boy as well. Denis's cold had got worse. He was running a temperature, and Goderich promised to come again next day.

Reports, then, on the two patients were discouraging. As for Raoul, – he had had to be moved to a small attic bedroom. His wound was an ugly one, and I somehow gathered an impression that Goderich was puzzled by the case.

Denis, it seemed probable, would not be fit to return punctually to school and for a time I half suspected him of shamming in order to postpone the parting with his friend. He, Denis, had been told of Raoul's misadventure and pleaded, vainly, to be allowed to see him. The pair were upon different floors, and in different wings, – the farther from each other, I had thought, the better.

Raoul's accident (and he could or would not state which dog or dogs it was that had attacked him) had been upon a Thursday, and by the Sunday his arm still showed no improvement. The following morning, Goderich rather surprised me by asking me to 'see for myself,' and I watched him unwrap the bandages. I caught, I fancied, an expression of something approaching astonishment on his face when the torn flesh was bared. The entire limb below the elbow was swollen and had a repulsive livid hue. Goderich motioned me to go. 'I'll see you afterwards,' he murmured.

'Well,' he said, rejoining me downstairs, 'I'll confess I'm

a bit foxed. The latest wonder-drug's proved a flop and – It's – It's quite extraordinary, but the whole fore-arm seems – '

'Yes, what?' I pressed impatiently.

'Why, to have mortified. But it – it *couldn't* have, to that extent, without other associated symptoms, gross symptoms, which just aren't there. Yet – well – Pah . . . ! Well, the damn thing almost stinks . . . !'

I stared at him, and he went on. 'I'm speaking unprofessionally, Habgood, and not merely being nosey. Precisely how you came by this odd customer I'm not enquiring, but – '

Our talk was interrupted by a scurrying commotion in the passage. The door burst open and Clara entered with scarcely a preliminary knock. 'Oh . . . excuse me, Sir, but – Master Denis – '

Behind her, at that instant, Denis himself appeared, tearfully distraught.

'What is it?' I said, pushing Clara aside and catching him up in my arms. 'What's happened?'

But for a while, after I had carried him back to bed, he refused to tell us. It was only, at first, from Clara that we discovered that Raoul must have stealthily crept from his room, traversed the intervening corridors, and visited the boy. Clara had heard a cry from within the bedroom and seen Raoul emerging just as she arrived upon the scene.

Furious, I was starting off there and then for Raoul's attic, but Goderich restrained me. 'Let me,' he said. 'I'll go.'

He was away a long time, and when he returned his words further amazed me.

'Well . . . I give up. I'm not a doctor. Doctors don't see such things. . . . Call me a bald-headed Belgian and be done with it. . . . I give it up!'

'What do you mean?'

'Why, when I got there, the fellow was smiling – by the

way, has he a face to smile with? I'm never sure – . . . was sort of smiling and holding out his arm and saying '*guéri, guéri,*' like a Cheshire cat . . . if they do . . . I – I'm a bit overcome. . . .'

'You mean – ?'

'I mean that it *was* cured, *is* cured. A little swelling, and he's a normal slight fever. Here, gimme a tot of your Glenlivet. . . . I tell you, I give up.'

This episode, itself grotesque, marked the beginning of a fresh, more ominous phase in my relationship with Raoul, and brought into my mind's open a host of doubts and until then but dimly realised fears. Just as the startled eye may all at once perceive the latent shapes of horror in the far, nobly drifting clouds and summer leaves, or as the meek familiar pattern of a wallpaper may spring into a sudden tracery of hell, so now the course of these events revealed a darker trend. The unaccountable affair of Raoul's arm had left me quite uncertain what to believe or disbelieve or what might happen next.

Circumstances had forced me to admit Goderich to my confidence, yet for a while we each fought shy of a direct discussion. What had occurred was so fantastically out of line with ordinary experience that we had, I suppose, to try somehow to deny and to discredit it a little even to ourselves.

Raoul made a complete recovery, and my determination to evict him was renewed. Denis however remained by no means well and I still shrank from distressing him. As if guessing what I meditated he had grown louder than usual in his companion's praises.

'You don't like him,' he accused, reproachfully yet with a suppressed tight smile that had about it – how shall I express it? – a sort of odd repugnant coyness.

'I – well, I just don't see anything much *in* him. . . . He can't stay here forever.'

'Why, what harm does he do? I *wish* you liked him '

I did not answer and we turned presently to other topics, but I continued baffled and, in some deeper sense, dismayed. It might be, as Denis said, that Raoul appeared to do no active harm, but it was this very negativity that partly was the trouble and made his evident attraction for my boy so utterly incomprehensible. The fellow, in his coarse labourer's clothes and ridiculous mittens, was an incongruity and an excrescence on the English countryside, – and yet his most outstanding characteristic, to be paradoxical, was his characterlessness. He seemed as sinisterly unresponsive and empty of emotion as a robot.

The date when Denis should have returned to school was passed. He had got better, then had a relapse, developing a variety of low undulant fever. An X-ray of his chest reassured me as to the state of his lungs, but the symptoms did not abate.

I was disappointed also in finding it, now, the harder to give Raoul his *congé*, – and I could not but connect the two things in my mind. Raoul, I was certain, was somehow the cause of Denis's poor appetite, his wan and wasted look, and alternating fits of nervous stimulation and depression. Denis slept in a room close to mine, and once or twice I fancied I heard noises of bumping and what I could then only describe as a kind of dull sustained metallic humming coming from it. A dark suspicion visited me. Could Raoul be there? But on softly opening the door I found Denis alone and apparently asleep. The noises, if there had been any, had entirely ceased.

However, and recalling the anomaly – or prodigy – of the instantaneously healed arm, I remained still convinced that Raoul must be, ultimately, their author.

This instinct or persuasion – that Raoul was the source of some pernicious influence destructive of my boy – gained steady strength. Denis's manner to me had changed, and his constant terror that I should part him from his strange playmate was obvious. While, more specifically, the noises I had heard *were* noises, I would swear it. They increased towards midnight but for a time, whenever I approached, died down.

Goderich, up to a point, did what he could, but was, I felt, as well aware as I that tonics and cough mixtures did not touch the matter's root. At last, after I had told him of the odd sounds, he remarked, mildly: 'If I were you, Habgood, I *would* consider getting rid of that chap "Raoul," you know . . . I really would.'

The restraint of this recommendation was almost comical, but I did not smile.

'Do you know anything *about* him? I was just wondering if, by any chance, he had ever had anything to do with your wife's family, – worked for them once maybe, and used that as an introduction to you? I'm only guessing. . . .'

'Oh, no,' I replied confidently enough. 'Denis chummed up with the beauty in the Vaignons' village in Auvergne, that's all.'

'These noises, – is there ever anything broken or disarranged as well, after you hear them?'

'No, I've – Wait a bit though . . .' Yes, I remembered, I *had* found a vase smashed once, and more than once had noticed drawers pulled out, and a general air of untidiness or confusion. I told Goderich so.

'Well, pass the word if that sort of thing hots up. And, seriously, I *should* give that chap the boot. It'll upset the lad, but – I should risk it.'

When Goderich had gone I pondered his indubitably sound advice lugubriously. I could readily guess what had been at the back of his mind in asking, as to the noises, whether anything had been broken or moved about, – yet the notion of poltergeist activities, while certainly sufficiently unpleasant, did not appear, entirely, to fit the case. They might, for all I knew, be present but, even so, would fall short of providing a complete explanation.

For, possibly, the hundredth time I vowed that Raoul *must* go; and indeed, quite apart from my own resolutions, matters were coming to a head. The commotions in Denis's room increased, being heard now by the servants, and were at last admitted by Denis himself. He denied all responsibility for them – in which I fully believed him – but did not seem afraid of, or disturbed by, them.

'But don't they wake you up and spoil your rest?'

'Oh . . . sometimes. But I don't care. I go to sleep again.'

He looked restive under my interrogation. Nowadays, he was dressed and intermittently able to stroll out of doors if it were sunny, but spent much of his time in a *chaise-longue*, either in his room or, latterly, with Raoul, on a glass-roofed verandah. The pair would sit there, conversing softly, the man whittling sticks which he would fashion into a variety of uncouth doll, and my boy watching him, fascinatedly, as if the world's fate hung upon these operations.

Denis glanced up at me appealingly. 'Promise me something.'

'What?' But I guessed what it would be.

'That – that you won't send Raoul away.'

'Well, as I've said already, he can't stay forever. Why do you think I shouldn't send him away?'

Denis's eyes, wide in some secret conjuring of disaster, met mine squarely. 'It would kill me,' he said simply.

As well as I might, although, I felt, evasively and with some sacrifice of honesty, I pacified him, and then left him. What *could* I do? Denis, of course, had been exaggerating and distraught, – but such words, from a child . . . !

Of late, he had grown appreciably thinner, and I had only to contrast these waxen cheeks and pallid lips with his comparatively vigorous appearance a short month ago to realise the alarming swiftness of the change. To say I could not *prove* this due to Raoul was idle. It was from Raoul's arrival that the symptoms dated, and it was from him, I was certain, that they sprang. This lay-figure – this *fantôche*, this hollow puppet – was the unhallowed instrument of a vile infestation that had assaulted Denis's whole physical and moral organism. . . . Watching the two together (as I was often able from a window overlooking the verandah) I would be driven into a kind of agony of speculation as to the nature of the bond between them. My boy's face, raptly brooding or wearing that charmed smile I loathed even more, was usually averted, but I caught on it, sometimes, an enthralled abandon or absorption that would chill my blood. The creature Raoul, meanwhile, in his adorer's presence, would seem re-animated, made less neuter and less negative, as if his very being were enhanced and – how to put it? – as if it were at Denis's expense, by Denis's depletion of vitality, that he existed or that his actuality was heightened, – as if, as the one waxed, the other shrank and waned. . . . Scarcely troubling to hide my agitation as such ideas possessed me, I had tried, once or twice, to break in upon the pair in these ambiguous intimacies, but, I soon recognised, to no avail. The two would fall momentarily silent, Denis looking half guilty and half angry; then, as I knew, the instant that my back was turned their curious *tête-à-tête* would recommence.

Nevertheless, despite its accumulating worry and distraction, my life had still preserved a surface ordinariness and normality. Friends would occasionally drop in on me, or I on them, as heretofore, – and I do not think, now, that they noticed much amiss. To be sure, they commented upon Denis's exhausted, drooping air and sympathised with my anxiety about him, but they can have seen little of Raoul, and probably the 'gossip' I had tended to imagine rife was confined chiefly to my own household.

There, certainly, there must have been some. Clara and old Jenny, even while not appreciating its significance, could not be blind (and deaf) to a good deal of what was happening under their noses, and their refusal to spread tales or 'fuss' was testimony to their loyalty and long-suffering discretion.

As for Raoul's outward or official status, this had been regularised with less ado than I expected. A week or so after his arrival, on the insistence as I learned surprisedly of Denis, he had gone into Winchester and, Denis acting as interpreter, registered at the police station as an alien.

'What did he put himself down as?' I had asked disturbedly. 'Not as my employee, I hope.' And 'Oh, no,' Denis reassured me. 'Just as a visitor. Just as your guest.' That sounded well enough and I had grudgingly had to give Denis credit for his enterprise, but to confirm it I went in myself next day to Winchester. Yes, everything, I was told, was quite in order; oh yes, perfectly. . . . I would have been interested to see the passport which must have been produced by Raoul, but had not pressed the matter.

I was recalling this piece of compliance with legalities – comfortingly factual and satisfactory-seeming so far as it went – to Goderich.

''M . . . ,' he mused dubiously. 'The blighter's an infernal incubus whatever else he is or ain't, and I wish you could just show him the door. As I've confessed, I'm a finger or so out of my depth. . . . The case is fairer game I fancy for a psychical researching bloke, or a psychiatrist. You're prejudiced, I realise, against *them*, and I'm not insisting, but – I'm worried about *you*, as well as Denis. I'll have two patients here, instead of one, directly. . . .'

It was true that the business was wrecking me. Each day, I felt that I could stand no more and that, to end it, I should be driven to some act of violence.

When I, eventually, *was* so driven it appeared, for a short time, almost a relief.

The situation had continued to deteriorate. Denis, after a session with his dear, would wear an aspect veritably of the grave, and the idea which had been shaping in my mind before besieged me now with an increasing force. He is losing something, giving something, I thought, but he would not *want* to do that, do it deliberately, more or less voluntarily, for nothing. He must get something, be tempted by something, in return, – but what, – ah, what?

I lived in a waking nightmare, and the idea's hold on me grew stronger. That Denis's delicately nurtured boyhood should fall prey to the appetites of an amorphous doll and become the meat of this uncanny zany seemed of all things the most abominable. The details and precise technique of such infernal commerce were beyond my fathoming, but that the ghastly trade existed and that Denis was its dedicated victim I felt positive. *Who* was this 'Raoul'? When he had first arrived I had attempted, if simply in grudging 'common courtesy,' to engage him in conversation, but his thick Auvergnat dialect (as I presumed it) had defeated me, and nowadays I did not try to talk with him. As I watched him through the window, whittling his sticks and looking rather like a well-fed scarecrow, a speechless rage possessed me. Was the man knave or loon? For hours on end, complacently yet dully and only his hands moving, he would squat there, with the bland corpulence and mindless sedentary persistence of some gigantic blow-fly, – and my own hands would writhe in fury. 'If I could catch him at it,' I thought chokingly, ' – if I could catch him at it I would strangle him. . . .'

'*If* I could catch him' . . . Yes . . . I had, emotionally, a very vague and general notion or suspicion of what might be going on, but that was all. While, as for 'evidence' . . . If this dumb, gangrened oaf were a variety of psychic leech as I surmised, able to tap and suck away my boy's vitality, his health and spiritual stamina, how was it done? It was probably, I realised, a vain or at least not ordinarily answerable question, – yet the business, I argued, must have some sort of 'rationale,' some sort of place and time. During a good part of the day the pair were under – or liable, if I chose, to come under – my observation, and I hardly believed that Denis received his consort in his bedroom, or vice versa. Latterly, Raoul had returned to his old sleeping-quarters in the loft, and in any case I had taken, I considered, adequate precautions against a nocturnal meeting. It was, however, then – between dusk and midnight – that the 'noises' and other disturbances were most troublesome; and this too, I reflected, fitted in with my 'theory' to some extent. Poltergeists, I had heard, were regarded as the prankish play of a surplus vital force or energy; and it was just after this force's flow, from Denis, had been stimulated but yet deprived, temporarily, of its accustomed receptacle in Raoul that the impish manifestations, centering round my boy, were commonest. As to the poltergeists themselves, if poltergeists they were, I was not primarily concerned about or bothered by them, – and it was commentary enough upon the situation, as I saw it, that such a matter should be reckoned a mere minor and subsidiary nuisance.

Could it be only – how long? – barely five weeks today, since 'Raoul' appeared. . . . ?

At this time, my nights were as a rule dark stretches of tormented wakefulness, and when – not, often, till towards early morning – I did fall asleep, my rest would usually be broken, and haunted by appalling dreams.

One of these I especially remember.

I was in France, and Cécile was still with me. She had been recounting, it seemed, a legend of her native province and, with an unexplained urgency, was directing my attention to a particular passage in a book. We were both standing by a wide window, and the diabolically piled Silurian landscape of Auvergne stretched from us, for many leagues, under a breathless summer heat. But the odd thing was that Cécile was holding the book up in front of her face, and expecting me to read it *through* its covers and all the intervening pages! This, in some miraculous manner, I was able, in my dream, to do, though with difficulty and a sense of growing apprehension and oppression. Of one sentence, which she was extraordinarily anxious I should read, I could make out four words only: '. . . shall feast upon the . . .' I was on the point, I thought, of deciphering the rest when suddenly the book slipped from my wife's hands, revealing, not her face, but – empty air. With a cry of terror, I awoke.

The dream *was* only a dream, and probably, just before I fell asleep, my mind had again been running on Goderich's query, once, as to a possible connection between Raoul and Cécile's family; yet its tense, loaded flavour clung to me, and had the quality, somehow, of a presentiment.

I felt I had no need to ask of what. For a good while now I had been scarcely capable of keeping up the pretence of normal living, and a crisis would not be long delayed. 'If I could catch him at it,' I found myself always repeating, 'If I could catch him. . . .'

And then, one day, I did.

It was an afternoon in October and Denis had been sitting, with his inseparable companion, on the sun-porch. Occasionally, he would desist from his talking and take up a book. It was a child's book from the shelves of his old nursery, and I was mildly surprised that he should still be interested in what I thought he had outgrown.

The verandah, as I have said, was glass-topped, and there was a glass-paned wind-break at one end too. Branches of a wisteria tree at the side had been persuaded to straggle irregularly over part of the roof, and there were pots of hydrangeas along the front. The blooms, now, were past their best, but the place retained a faded greenness and a, to me, pleasantly shabby, half-neglected air which I should have been sorry to see give way to greater trimness.

A window, as I have also said, commanded a restricted view of this semi-enclosed space, and it was through this window (the high French window of a small spare parlour) that I had often, with an uneasiness that had mounted, as the weeks dragged by, to anguish, watched my boy and his companion. Yet what was the good of that, I asked myself? They must realise, by this, my bursting suspicions and antagonism, and, to them, my harrowed glances would be merely 'spying.' Denis was alienated from me – from his own father – and there was nothing I could do.

On this afternoon I quickly abandoned such entirely fruitless surveillance. I must find something to occupy my thoughts and hands or else go mad, and I had remembered a broken fence by the apple orchard that needed mending. But, having collected hammer and nails, I had scarcely started on my job before a fearful premonition of disaster gathered in my brain. I was aware, as if by a direct insight, of something enormously, incredibly evil. I must go back. . . . This recognition of sheer calamity was so overpowering that I instantly dropped my tools and actually started running towards the house.

However, an instinct of discretion slowed my steps and I approached more cautiously. I could not, where I was, be seen from the verandah but, to make doubly sure, I took a devious route around a hedge of macracarpa. Mingled with my apprehension was a swelling rage. How could I have been so blind, I remember thinking, to what was going on under my nose? For that was what it had amounted to. Why had I fancied that this infernal traffic necessarily required a set 'rendezvous,' or any physical propinquity? 'I will strangle him,' I heard myself saying. 'He deserves it and I shall do it.' It was as if my fingers were upon the creature's neck, as if time were foreshortened or in some fashion telescoped, as if what was to happen had already happened and I was already there. . . .

The October day was waning as, very quietly, I re-entered the parlour, tip-toed across the room, and looked.

Raoul, from where I stood, was invisible, but I could see Denis plainly, still sitting, as I had left him, in a battered old wicker chair, reading his book. Or rather, he was not so much 'sitting' as crouching, hunched forward in an odd stiff posture on the edge of the chair-seat. A last shaft of reddening light drew frail fire from his blonde hair, but his face was hidden by the book.

An intimation of horror and of an unnameable corruption filled my heart. Something in Denis's queer locked attitude, in his whole appearance, utterly dismayed and sickened me.

Hardly breathing, I stole nearer. My movement was very soft, but Denis must have caught or have divined it, for he started violently. The book slipped from his hands.

Upon his suddenly revealed face was an expression I will not describe. It was open before me, like a dreadful flower. Evil, we know, exacts it dues of ruin from the tenderest transgressors, but the reverse side of the matter is less willingly admitted and more shocking; and now the swift unveiling for me of sin's fleeting wage to my unhappy boy was beyond words appalling.

I would, if I could, have shut my eyes on what I had surprised. Denis's features, fixed in their long enchantment, wore a look that was a travesty of boyhood and a blasphemy of all my memories of him. The face, in its ecstasy, was laced and hemmed, and old, with an oldness that had nothing to do with years. Watching him, while the running sands of his being received their frightful recompense, I too was a prisoner to an unreal eternity, though in my case of anguish.

Then, instantaneously, the spell was broken, as Denis gave a low despairing cry. I flung apart the French windows and dashed on to the verandah.

Where was Raoul? Denis, I must subconsciously have told myself, would recover presently from his half-swoon and my first business was with his despoiler. Had the thing vanished? Not altogether. Below the verandah, in the direction of the shrubbery, I indistinctly glimpsed it, already in lumbering flight.

I caught it up beside the hedge of macracarpa, making for the coach-house. The figure, shadowy in the fading light, had turned at my approach and in an odd ineffective way put up a fumbling arm to keep me off.

My hands closed round its throat and for a while we struggled, swaying. Some seconds passed, and as yet the loathsome ninny had remained quite silent, but, all at once, I heard a little noise. It is said that certain creatures, ordinarily voiceless, may, in extremity, find feeble tongue – that, in the agony of boiling, wretched lobsters compass a last faint unexampled squeak – and it was, now, of such a puny cry that I was put in mind. The sound filled me with revulsion.

My fingers pressed more strongly. Raoul, as we grappled, was being forced slowly backwards towards a tree-trunk, against which it was my idea to pin him and –

Either he had managed to trip me, or I had slipped and stumbled. The two of us crashed heavily, I uppermost. For some seconds longer I was still aware of him beneath me, writhing and battling, yet, somehow, eluding me; but the next moment, he had gone.

Dazedly, I picked myself up and gazed round me in search of the thing that had melted into vacancy from my grasp; and there was no sign of it, anywhere at all.

II

THEY were black days that followed – I cannot convey *how* black. Though, with the exit of Denis's sinister playfellow, the worst seemed over, I felt in my heart, chilly, that this was only an uneasy breathing-space and that the story, yet, was far from done.

'Breathing-space' – no, it was not really even that. Raoul, I hoped, was banished, but his work remained. Denis was ill. Staring at me with horror and aversion, as if *I* were the sole author of his misery, he could scarcely bear that I should speak to him or go near his bed. The loss, I recognised with anguish, of his frightful parasite and paramour had virtually prostrated him, and he had ceased to be the boy Cécile and I had loved.

As to the eerie lummox who had plagued us – I concluded that he had succeeded, somehow, in wriggling free from me and fleeing, that he would probably make his way back to France, and that, at least in person (if he *were* a person) he would trouble us no more. Or rather, this was what I tried to tell myself I had concluded. Truth is not necessarily or always 'sober,' and there was something here, I realised inwardly, of which all ordinary 'sane' explanations and conjectures failed to take account.

Denis, when I had re-entered the house after Raoul's flight, had been in a half-faint. The servants, roused by my running footsteps along the verandah, had found him lying by the chair, and carried him to his room. Reviving, he had set up a low continuous moaning which did not abate till Goderich, whom I had at once rung up, had given him a sedative. That had secured him a night's sleep; but next day, as I have said, he would hardly suffer my approach, and once had even barricaded his door against me. I was at my wit's end, and terrified lest he should do himself an injury.

Goderich shared my anxiety.

'Have you discovered any more about this unholy creature, now he's gone?' he asked.

' "Any more?" Why, how – '

'I mean that, now he *has* gone, tongues might wag a bit more freely. Your servants', for instance. . . .'

'Oh, yes,' I agreed. 'Yes . . . plenty of that!'

It was a fact that Jenny and Clara had unbosomed themselves to me of a good deal as to Raoul and their sentiments towards him which they had hitherto repressed – though without adding materially to my actual information. I told Goderich so.

'How did you explain the fellow's sudden disappearance to them?'

'I didn't. In any detail. They must have guessed that I – well, chased him off. I don't think they cared how he went, as long *as* he went.'

' 'M . . . Well, honestly, I feel I can't do much. I wish you *would* try a psychiatrist. . . .'

But I was not ready for that, yet. And was there, possibly, an ever so slightly hurt or reproachful tone in my friend's voice? If so, it must have been because he could divine that with him too, in my description of the final scene, I had been reticent of what I had called 'details'. . . .

Denis recovered to the extent of leaving his bed and room and occasionally loitering, alone, about the orchard and the meadow; but we were strangers to each other. My acquaintance, or partial acquaintance, with his dreadful secret made me a terror to him, and there seemed something pathetically horrible in the evident efforts of this child to wrest the situation to his own partisan, extenuating view of it – to digest, modify or soften it so as to render it more tolerable to him, and to see me, not Raoul, as his enemy.

It could not, I would think, go on like this. How, if I lived to be a hundred, could I forget – or *he* forget that I must still remember? I would remind him always. As he grew up, if not already, in a shame so poignantly embarrassed, he would wish my death. . . .

Thus, for a week or so, matters continued. My uncertainty as to what had really happened to Raoul prevented my finding much consolation even in his absence, and soon after his disappearance I had a visit from the Winchester City police. 'Privache,' they said (at first I barely recalled the fellow's surname) had failed to report at the expiration of one month's residence – and was he with me still? I could only reply, with a modicum of truth, that he had run off suddenly, I had no notion where. '"Run off?"' 'Yes.' I explained that the defaulter was a friend of my boy's of whom I had practically no knowledge; and I could see that my worthy – and, to me, very respectful – constable was dissatisfied and puzzled. 'He should 'a checked out properly,' he grumbled. 'If 'e went back to France, now, there'd be trouble and an 'itch, you see, o' some kind, at the port.'

Meanwhile the improvement in Denis's condition had been, at least superficially, maintained. That was, he looked a shade less pale and had a better appetite. The nightly thumpings, hummings and (a new ingredient) derisive hootings had, however, increased, the racket finally attaining such proportions that, out of consideration for my domestics' rest, I had his bedroom changed to one as far from theirs as possible.

To me, his manner remained stubbornly hostile. I had pleadingly attempted to get him to speak openly, frankly and give me his own version of affairs, but quite in vain. It seemed but too apparent that he had suffered a veritable bereavement and was still pining for his vanished mate. Reluctantly, I was beginning to resign myself to taking Goderich's advice and trying a psychiatrist. This course would pretty evidently expose me, as well as the patient proper, to a good deal of awkwardness and incredulous silly catechisings, but I must shirk no measure that might restore my boy.

The leaves were falling and the October days growing colder when I happened to receive a note reminding me of the approaching anniversary dinner of my old regiment. I had never missed attending it, and the formal invitation card was enclosed, but now I had no heart to go, and besides it would be out of the question. On the other hand, it was from Winchester, barely six miles away, that Mayfield, who had been my adjutant and was organising the affair this year, had written me. He chanced, he told me, to be spending the inside of a week there on business – and he was probably expecting, I surmised, that I should ask him to stay with me instead of at his hotel, at any rate for Saturday and Sunday.

This too, as matters were, was scarcely practicable, but the least I could do, I thought, was to run over to Winchester and see him. I decided to risk leaving Denis in Jenny's and Clara's care, and drove off after lunch.

My chat with Mayfield, to whom I explained the position so far as necessary, was as pleasant as anything could be in my state of worry about Denis, but I hurried home from it so as to arrive by tea-time.

Clara and Jenny, to my dismay, were both waiting for me at the porch, and their first words, as I jumped out of the car, told me the worst.

Denis had gone.

Self-reproach was as useless as unavoidable. I had to act.

'When did you miss him?' I asked.

It had been only twenty minutes ago. He had been on the verandah, and then, no longer seeing him there and wishing to reassure themselves, they had looked for him. His room was empty, and fairly tidy, but a small suitcase was undiscoverable, likewise some socks and a shirt. The most conclusive piece of evidence, however, which seemed to rule out hope that he had merely set off for a walk and might return, was the fact that Jenny's room also had been entered, and her money stolen.

'How much?'

'Four pounds ten, Sir. I – I had it in a little china box and was going to bank it Tuesday.'

Expecting me at any moment, they had not as yet given an alarm to the police, and I decided, rather than telephone, to drive back again myself to Winchester. Meanwhile, Jenny could ring me at the police station if my poor truant did, after all, return.

The desk sergeant knew me well and listened attentively to my story. 'It's early yet,' he encouraged, 'and he *may* be just – just larking. But of course we'll notify it and alert other stations round about. Five-fifteen now. . . . He can't be very far.'

'And watch the ports too,' I reminded him. My first thought, naturally, had been of Raoul, and my first fear that Denis was rejoining him.

'Oh, yes, we'll do that, as routine – although he couldn't get across, you know, without a passport.'

As to that I had, privately, my doubts. Given sufficient determination, there *were* ways of doing it, as a recent instance happened to have shown.

After a further consultation – this time with the local superintendent in his adjoining sanctum – I drove home.

'No news, I suppose, Jenny?'

'No, Sir.'

With what fortitude we could we resigned ourselves, as

remorseful empty hours passed, to the wretched, and in my case almost sleepless, night.

Feeling that the emergency had more than justified my breaking any rule of silence, I sent a wire of enquiry to M. Vaignon. An answer arrived, fairly promptly: 'Not here yet.'

This left me more 'up in the air' than ever, and in vain did I strive to supply, as it were, the real and un-telegraphable intonation of that word 'yet.' It sounded as if M. Vaignon rather expected that Denis *might* come, later – but I could not be sure.

I returned to the question of the passport. Denis *had* had a passport – an individual one, to allow of his escort sometimes by Flébard and sometimes by myself. But I had locked it up after his last trip, and had it locked up still. In any case, I thought, he must have realized that, before he could possibly reach the coast, the dock police would have been warned, so that the document would be useless to him.

The Winchester district, I was told, had been combed thoroughly without result and, as time passed, it surprised me that a boy could elude the police net for so long. It argued, certainly, either a degree of ineptitude on the one side or considerable adroitness and resource upon the other. Perhaps, whatever official incredulity might say, Denis had succeeded, by walking only at night and spending each day up a tree (in a manner I had read of) in striking a place where French fishing-boats put in, and then bribed some sailor into smuggling him across. . . .

This notion was if anything strengthened by a discovery made by Clara when the hunt was six days old. She ran excitedly to me in my study one morning, crying: 'Oh, we've – we've found something!'

It transpired that, in cleaning out the loft, she had come upon two loaves, two tins of sardines and a can-opener, a jar of marmalade *and* the suit-case, which was empty – a veritable *cache*!

These objects, which I went with her to inspect, had been hidden under sacking near a back door giving on to a short outer stair by which access could be gained to the loft without first passing through the coach-house below. Close by, I noticed with aversion, was a collection of the grotesque wooden dolls, something like ninepins, which Raoul had been used to whittle, and – most significantly – an empty opened tin and scattered crumbs showed that one meal at least had been consumed up there already.

However illogically, this find, and particularly the abandoned suit-case, established as an emotional certainty in my mind the belief that Denis had managed to reach France, or was upon his way there. He had been clever enough, I told myself, to lie hidden in the immediate vicinity while the search was most intensive, and then to slip off by night as I had supposed. Yes, that was it – that must be it! I came to a prompt decision.

That very afternoon, having rung Goderich to tell him what I contemplated, I set off for Southampton, calling in at the Winchester police station *en route*. I could see that my plan to 'pursue' (they would not admit that it *was* that) my boy to France had met with official scepticism and disfavour, but – though I did concur in the suggestion that a watch be set, if all too tardily, around the loft – I would not allow the cold water thrown on it to weaken my resolve.

And, as it happened, while I was not to know it then, I had only as it were anticipated matters by a single night. A second wire from M. Vaignon, I learned later, 'Denis here,' arrived for me the morning after I had left.

Once more, the prosaic and accustomed train, my gently heaving bunk upon the almost as accustomed channel packet, and the familiar harbour of Le Havre at misty dawn. The same, yes all the same, and yet how different! Many times had I made this crossing, but with a heart unracked, as now, by care.

Eating my *petit déjeuner* in the station buffet when I had passed through the customs, I bought a newspaper and a further supply of brioches and again boarded the train.

Paris and lunch, then southwards – on to what? As we began to breast the gradual ascent towards the *massif* a vague but dreadful apprehension grew upon me. I had dashed off from England, I realised, largely because inaction had become intolerable – yet here, in France, I quailed. It was as if, while I approached that black and tortured landscape of Auvergne, I were adventuring foolhardily into some citadel of evil powers, pitting my puny strength against a host of devils.

I took up my newspaper and tried to read – in vain. Denis, I thought, where are you? What are you doing now – and why?

With an effort, I forced myself to re-examine, as critically and calmly as I might, the chain of circumstances that had led to my being where I was, and upon such a quest.

Vaignon – and Raoul. . . . The whole business of the holiday exchanges had been so casual, so benign, and yet – yes. . . . There must be some connection, beyond mere coincidence, between the two.

I recalled M. Vaignon's brooding and half-guilty looks – and that peculiar scrap of conversation I had overheard. 'It has *come again*,' he had said then to Flébard. What had 'come again?' Could it –

Suddenly my mind snapped on something, and deliberately, for a second, I made it blank, as if afraid of the light that threatened all at once to flood it. I even grabbed my paper and feigned a furious engrossment in its long columns of advertisements. Next moment, however, I gave up the pretence, and a sigh escaped me – a sort of cold sigh of recognition and admission. 'Could it – ?' Why yes, of course it could. The 'It' of M. Vaignon's terrified lament was – Raoul.

How this lurking while fairly obvious conjecture had managed to get itself hushed up in the recesses of my brain (as I am sure it had) for such a time before issuing forth at last to startle me I did not know. But I found it, now, a highly disturbing one. Without, as yet, being able to appreciate all its implications I felt, dimly, a kind of spreading illumination, as though the contours of some formidable truth would presently emerge.

To reach Foant I had, directly, to change to a slower train, with a number of stops. The countryside remained, on the whole, placidly pastoral, but I fancied I began to detect in it, here and there, faint earnests or intimations of that sinister quality which the Auvergne whither I travelled had always held for me. M. Vaignon would be prepared for my coming, since I had telegraphed him from Le Havre, but what sort of welcome he would accord me I had no idea. I had not, it must be remembered, received the wire from him that would arrive at 'Ashtoft' the next morning, and I had nothing, at the moment, but my impulsive intuition to lead me to suppose Denis at the château.

The sun was westering as we slackened speed for Foant, and before that, of course, the scenery had assumed the intimidating gigantism and cataclysmic look of violence which, every time I visited the place, had sent a shiver up my spine.

Alighting, I stared round me but could see no one, on my own island platform or on either of the other two, except the ticket collector and a couple of peasant women.

Perhaps M. Vaignon was so indignant at my flat defiance of his previous virtual prohibition that he was not sending anyone to meet me! Owing to his strange imposition of silence I had felt unable to write to him – or question him maybe concerning Raoul – and though I now suspected him of knowing more about it than he might confess his official state was one of ignorance, and he might not appreciate the seriousness of the case.

For a quarter of an hour I waited impatiently in the little *salle d'attente*. Had M. Vaignon actually resolved to deny me his hospitality? But no; he *had* answered my first wire, and surely, in common humanity, he couldn't be such a bear – and such a brute!

I was however on the point either of telephoning the château or, without doing so, of hiring, if I could, a taxi, when a car hurtled furiously into the station yard. It hurtled in *so* furiously that I experienced a curious start of anticlimax at sight of the form that crawled feebly out from the driving-seat.

The figure advanced immediately, with a sort of frenzied impetuous hobble, towards me.

Yes, it was M. Vaignon.

III

QUESTION and answer between us tumbled over each other, standing on no ceremony of greeting. 'Is he with you?'

'Yes . . . but you could not have my telegram so soon.'

'Is he – all right?'

'He – you will see. . . .'

We got into the car. 'Flébard,' M. Vaignon explained interjectorily, 'has left, and it is I who am chauffeur. I fear I am late.'

I mumbled something, to which he paid no attention. We had shot out of the station yard into the gathering dusk of the highway, M. Vaignon still driving like a maniac. His manner, notwithstanding, had a kind of distrait, debonair moroseness, and the conditions generally, as we careened wildly onwards, were unfavourable to conversation. Yet I did, once, attempt it. 'Denis has been terribly ill,' I said. 'He is not himself, or he would not have run away, and I would not have had to trouble you. How does he seem, now?'

M. Vaignon's nearer shoulder gave me an absent shrug. 'I cannot tell you. . . . We are all bedevilled, *n'est-ce pas*, and the evil days are on us. They are on your boy, who does not know you are here but won't, I bet you, let you talk to him, or get within ten feet of him. . . .'

My heart sank, but despair goaded me to a flare of anger too.

'We shall see about that!' I said.

The château, when we entered it at nightfall, was a

place of dark, uneasy stillness. A man whose face was unfamiliar had admitted us and he immediately retreated again from us.

'Where is Denis?' I asked M. Vaignon. 'Where is he?'

We had passed, from the hall, into a small salon to the left, wherein, I remembered, it had once been promised that Denis should devote a daily hour to the study of De Musset, the Dumas and Victor Hugo. Whether he had ever done so I doubted, but two walls of the room were book-lined.

'Where *is* he?' I repeated, but at this very instant, hearing a step along the hall, I glanced up towards the door, and there, staring back frozenly at me, was – Denis.

It was a glimpse only that I had of him for with a kind of indignantly affrighted '*Ah . . .*' he vanished. I rushed out after him into the hall, calling his name.

A man – it was he who had let us in – stood there. 'Dinner will be – ,' he was beginning.

'Where is my boy, *le jeune garçon*?' I interrupted him. 'Which way did he go just now? Which is his room?'

The fellow regarded me consideringly as he replied, slowly: 'The same . . . but – ' He stopped, then, with a quick and as if guilty or surreptitious movement, crossed himself.

Denis's old room was on the first floor, by the stair-head. Having run up to it, I tried the door, but it was locked and there was no answer to my knocks. 'Denis!' I cried. 'Denis, are you there?'

Not a sound. It was just possible though most unlikely that the door had been locked from the outside. I knocked and called again, in vain.

Descending to the salon, I debated, wretchedly. It appeared but too evident that M. Vaignon had spoken truly and that Denis had not ceased to regard me as his enemy. I recalled, in misery, the intonation of his '*Ah . . . !*' when he caught sight of me some moments since. It had been an 'Ah!' not merely of disconcertment and dismay but, I realized, of actual execration.

M. Vaignon had come out into the hall. 'You see,' he murmured dryly, 'I was right. . . .'

At dinner, no place was laid for Denis, and M. Vaignon must have noticed my disappointedly enquiring glances. In the presence, however, of the ever-attendant Dorlot (as, I gathered, was his name) nothing of any importance could be said, and our talk was of trivialities.

Meanwhile, my mind ran feverishly on what I had so far discovered. I had already seen, alas, enough to recognise that matters could not be adjusted offhand, or hurried, and that the home-bringing of my poor prodigal would prove no simple and probably no brief procedure. There would be difficulties, especially in a foreign country, about compelling him, forcibly, to go with me, and, in consulting with M. Vaignon and striving to come at the inner truth of the whole business, I must do what I could to practise greater patience and restraint.

After the meal I again followed M. Vaignon into the salon, where he motioned me to a seat by the fire.

'As you will doubtless have observed,' he began immediately, anticipating one, though certainly not the most pressing, of the questions that burned upon my tongue, 'Marcel and Augustine are gone. They were in all benevolence snatched from me by an aunt, my sister-in-law, who considered the atmosphere here not – not altogether sympathetic to young children . . . *Mon dieu*, ha, ha . . . how very right she was . . . !'

My good resolutions, at such words, broke down, and I burst out: 'And *my* child, *Monsieur*, what about *him*? He wasn't at dinner with us. Where is he *now*? Is he safe *now*, this minute . . . ? When did he come here, and why? You have told me nothing yet. There is a person, a creature, "Raoul," who – '

'*Ah, ça . . .*!' M. Vaignon had raised a nervously, or it may only have been contemptuously, deprecating hand to check me. 'Let us not speak that name too loudly! It is a name, to me, of ridicule and of annoyance; to others, many people, whose susceptibilities one must regard, of – well, of something infinitely worse. It – '

He paused, continuing presently: 'You are bound, now that you are here, to hear of this – this nonsense – anyhow, and I may just as well prepare you and forewarn you. . . . *Enfin* – it was of that, in fact, I wrote to you, or anyhow of that that I was thinking when I advised you in my letter not to send me your boy again. When I told you I was the victim of a persecution, as, in a mood of some exasperation, I recall I did, I was hardly exaggerating, and – '

'But,' I broke in, 'I don't understand how – ' I hesitated, for my most urgent question would not be repressed. 'Is he – is it – here now?'

M. Vaignon considered me warily. 'It – if we are to call this damnable old wives' tale an "it" – is not here, or active, now. That is to say – *enfin*, it is not here now. . . .'

After a moment he went on, morosely: 'As for "understanding" . . . There are things of which one can perceive the effect, upon oneself and others, but which one may not altogether "understand," and may indeed, in a sense, entirely repudiate. As I have just told you, this – this nuisance, this most supreme and consummate nuisance – is not with us, *actuellement*, but your boy – your boy arrived here late last night, in – in search of it. He is trying – he will do his best, to get it back. . . .'

It would be hard to describe the unhappy confusion into which these words had thrown me. What was I to believe? M. Vaignon had alluded almost scoffingly to Raoul as if to a sort of troublesome but relatively minor notifiable disease or garden pest – much as he might have spoken of some curiously periodic scarlatina or potato-blight! – yet underneath his shrugging air I could divine a genuine and continuing apprehension.

He rose abruptly, with an access of agitation. 'This thing – this kind of molestation, or superstition of a molestation – is not entirely unexampled if one may credit certain authors, certain bogeymongers, of – oh, of at least two centuries and more ago. . . .' He had moved to the bookshelves, ran a finger along the tops of a few heavy-looking tomes, and half pulled one out. 'No matter . . . ,' he said, pushing the volume into place again. 'It is there . . . and duly catalogued, though under an evasive appellation. They called these – these preposterousnesses, or the cast of mind that fostered and engendered them, '*sans noms*', – simply that. The "nameless" . . .'

Undecidedly, he resumed his seat. 'I – I give you my word of honour that, when I first met you and until recently, this particular – "nameless" had not, to my recognition, bothered us, or at all events. . . . I do not deny that it, or the – the rumour of it, was supposed to *have* bothered us in the past, but it was presumed to be gone. *Tant même*, there was a technical, an academic risk of which I might no doubt have warned you earlier. . . .'

A tide of bewildered anger swelled in me. 'Yes,' I said bitterly, ' "rumour" or not, whatever the thing was, and whether we are mad or sane, you might indeed! You certainly should have warned me!'

'Yet you would have laughed, and rightly or *au moins* most excusably, at such a history. You would have derided it and me.'

'And what would that have mattered if I *had*?' I almost shouted, unable longer to contain the explosion of impatience. I had had to wait, on tenterhooks, all through the drive from Foant and then through dinner to ask anything of what I had been bursting desperately to ask – and now, when I could at last demand straightforward answers, I was treated to nothing but side-steppings and prevarications.

M. Vaignon was silent, his head bowed. I was entirely convinced that he knew very well he had not told me the whole story and was still keeping something back.

'This – this "nameless," ' I insisted. 'What *is* it? I mean this particular specimen. . . . We are just beating round the bush about it all and I can't in the least follow what it really is you think you are telling me – if you *are* telling me. What *is* it? That's what I've got to know! But whatever it is you surely could have stopped my boy from – from meeting it. *He* told me it was someone he – chummed up with in the village. A kind of semi-vagrant, it sounded, but . . .'

My words trailed away. M. Vaignon, his face white under my accusation, twirled his brandy, of which a glass was before me too, untasted.

He raised his own glass all at once and drained it. His expression showed an almost morbid exaltation.

'*Ah, bah!* "It," you say, – "*it*" . . . ! *Eh bien*. . . . "*It*" is something, if you please, that ebbs and flows and that refuses to be satisfactorily dead, something that crops up and comes and goes, and is reputed to have plagued my family through three generations; something that has nourished itself, at intervals, so the tale runs, at our expense and owes its very being and persistence to its victims. All that – ha, ha! – is in the text-book. . . . Oh, we are not unique in this affliction. "The So-and-so's", you will hear, " – ah yes, a fine old family, *but* – they have a *sans-nom*. . . ." As for this – this particular example, as you say, it has a human shape, which you have seen. It eats, drinks, sleeps as other men, while it exists. *Mon dieu* . . . "it" has even mended my hedges, and bought soap or tea or salt at the *épicerie*, before I suspected it and till it was recognised. . . . And then, when it *was* recognised – oh what a how-d'ye-do . . . ! But, *to* exist, it must, they say, have an – an attachment. And – its attachment must be young. If and when its victim, its *petit ami*, dies, the pest transfers its – its attentions, we are to believe, to the children of another, and the nearest, branch. The thing is amorous and – and rapacious. *Ah, nom d'un nom, quelle histoire! Quel fumisterie! Quelle imbécilite! C'est ridicule, fantastique, incroyable . . . !*'

His voice had risen wildly on a note, it might be equally of scorn or terror as a knock, at first soft, then louder, was repeated on the door. The man Dorlot entered, wearing a look of remonstrance.

'*Monsieur* should know that such excitement, of which the noise has penetrated to the kitchen, is very bad for him. Go to bed, *Monsieur*, I advise it. Go to bed, where you may forget our troubles possibly in sleep.'

Meekly accepting the rebuke – and, I imagined, rather welcoming the excuse to escape further questioning – M. Vaignon said, to me: 'Dorlot is right, and, if you will forgive me, I shall leave you now. My health, latterly, is precarious. . . . Dorlot will give you anything you require. But first – ' he turned to the man – 'Where is the young *monsieur*? Is he in his room, and – and quiet?'

'Yes; he is in his room, as is to be inferred from the very fact that his room is *not* entirely quiet. The noises are there again, while not, as yet, excessive.'

My heart sank at these words, though they conveyed nothing new. The 'poltergeist' disturbances, however, were connected in my mind with Raoul, and their continuance depressed me.

'Good night . . . ,' said M. Vaignon.

I was desperately tired, but lingered a little longer in the 'library.'

What, honestly, could I believe, and what try, still, to disbelieve? Ordinarily, of course, the recital which my host had just concluded would be dismissible as a farrago of lurid and unpleasant nonsense – but I had had experience, alas, myself, of what too plainly contradicted this consoling view.

As I was going over what M. Vaignon had said, and sipping my brandy at last, my eye fell on the volume he had started to pull out from the shelves. It protruded slightly still, and I got up and took it to my seat.

Légendes d'Autrefois the tome was entitled, tritely, but I had scarcely flicked over a haphazard page or two before I read, as if my glance had been directed to the spot: '. . . *et, c'est à dire, les morts se régaleront des vivants. . . .*'

I experienced a cold grue of that sort of surprise which is not surprise at all, but eerie confirmation, and immediately restored the volume. 'The dead shall feast upon the living' . . . There it was, and I did not want, at present, to read more. It was the completion of the passage in that dream that I had had, some weeks ago, about my wife, holding the book before her nonexistent face. . . .

I don't know what had made me so optimistic, in leaving England, as to the prospect of an early return there with my boy. No doubt I had the legal right to compel him to come home, but if he still repulsed me and offered physical resistance the practical difficulties would be, to put it mildly, formidable. On the morning after my arrival and throughout that day and the next I had tried again to speak with him, but either his room would be locked and silent or, if I caught sight of him at all upon the stairs or in the grounds, he would take literally to his heels.

'Where does he eat?' I asked – for he continued absent from our meals – and it appeared that sometimes he would raid the larder and carry off his plunder to the fields. Neither M. Vaignon nor his domestics had any control over him, and, even if they had, I could not have relied on them to exercise it upon my behalf. As to the servants, they were in all respects so uncooperative as to be almost obstructionist, while, in particular, their extraordinary reticence caused me to think that they had probably been forbidden to 'gossip' with me, upon this or any other subject.

How fervently I wished that Goderich were here! But of course he could not desert his patients at short notice, nor, obviously, was M. Vaignon's hospitality in my gift.

Denis, I found, had done as I had thought and managed to stow away upon a fishing-boat at Brixham. It had been evidently useless for him to pretend that his visit had my sanction and he must have known I would eventually pursue him – but, beyond his infatuated determination to be reunited with Raoul at any cost, I doubted whether he could have had much of a settled plan of action and campaign. He had steered as clear as possible, it seemed, of M. Vaignon and so far as I could gather had confided the manner of his crossing only – half inadvertently – to Dorlot, who had retailed the story subsequently to his master.

Well it was a beautiful kettle of fish all round. I sent a wire to the police at Winchester, reflecting what slight satisfaction it had brought me thus to have proved them wrong.

In my anxiety, I had little or no help from M. Vaignon. Either he was genuinely ill, or feigned it to avoid my 'badgering.' Never joining me at breakfast, he would retire, though with excuses, immediately after lunch and dinner; and, since our talk on the first evening, had said nothing to me of the least seriousness, sincerity or moment as to what should have been our common problem.

Left to my own devices, I would wander wretchedly around the estate and nearer villages, exchanging a '*bonjour*' occasionally with some peasant, but often meeting no one, as I chose the less frequented paths. The autumn days were dull, but now and then a brighter spell invited me to extend my rambles towards a puy that topped a line of rocky hillocks to the north.

One afternoon – it was the fourth or fifth since my arrival – I had set out thither at about three o'clock. I paid no particular heed to where I was going, and walked on, I suppose, with my head bent in gloomy thought, for which I certainly had food enough.

Yes, the position was fantastic, and a description of it, given baldly, would provoke only pitying disbelief. And yet the history was *true*. That was, I knew that as much of it as I had seen with my own eyes was true. As for the rest – for M. Vaignon's wild while half-contemptuous elaborations on the theme – I reserved judgement. He was a sick man, whatever the cause, and his troubles seemed reflected in the unprosperous, depleted and decayed condition generally of his estate and household. The château was in disrepair and its staff, whether by flight or by dismissal, reduced to an uneasy remnant. Why, for example, had the trusted Flébard left? My heart was leaden with misgiving. Could M. Vaignon – a diabolic suspicion flashed into my brain – could he, initially, have asked Denis to the château, or anyhow have gone on having him there, in order to – to safeguard *his* children? Could he, at one time, to protect *them*, to divert something from them and fasten it on Denis, have actually been tempted to promote and foster the disastrous intimacy between Raoul and my boy . . . ? But I rejected such a vile hypothesis as altogether too far-fetched. My mind, as well, must be infected to have harboured it, and. . . .

Suddenly, rousing from my reverie, I looked about me. The country was unfamiliar and very lonely, and a small half-ruined church or chapel, with a graveyard attached, added to its general air of desolation. In that indifference of purpose which is born of mental exhaustion rather than of any, even 'idle,' curiosity, I entered the graveyard and wandered aimlessly among its tombs. Some distance off, I noticed, a man was wending towards me down the road ahead.

I loitered absently round the inside of the boundary wall. The burial-ground was evidently disused and the graves were untended, many overgrown with bramble or rank grass. Now and then a date caught my eye – 1830, 1813, 1770. . . . Possibly the – all at once I stopped, transfixed, as in the silence, a name stole, staring back at me. It was inscribed upon a headstone slightly taller than the rest, though lichen-coated, tilted, cracked and weather-worn as they. 'Privache.' . . . And, just decipherable below – yes. '*Raoul. Mourut 1873.*'

A footfall made me start. It was the man I had seen on the road and whose approach, over the grass, had been noiseless. He seemed a respectable, decent fellow of the sturdy 'bonhomme' type, probably a small tradesman or petty farmer – but he was regarding me, and the grave, with a frown of sombre disapproval.

He gave a significant upward jerk of the head and pointed to the tomb. '*Monsieur* knows perhaps of whom that is the grave?'

In a double disconcertment I stammered, faintly: 'Yes, I – I know the – no, I cannot, I – I mean it is the name, the same name as somebody's I know.'

The man took a step backward, crossed himself, and said, coldly: 'Enough . . . then it is to be hoped that *Monsieur* knows also that it is a bad name. . . . *Alors, bonjour, Monsieur.*'

He was going slowly away from me but, on an impulse, I detained him.

'Why, who – who was he?' I asked. 'Was he a – a criminal, or – '

My tongue faltered, and, as the man's glance met mine searchingly, it was as if a thousand things had passed wordlessly between us.

'No, *Monsieur*, in life he was not a criminal, but – .' He paused, then, stooping, traced with a forefinger the date, 1873. 'That, *Monsieur*, was when he died. It is there, cut in the stone, and is, so far as it goes, correct. My father was *maire* of the *commune* and could remember all about it. I have even, myself, seen the burial record, which was in the register of the parish, before the amalgamation. I can tell you no more than that, if you please, *Monsieur* – that he died almost eighty years ago, in 1873. . . .'

Again he crossed himself, and this time, as he withdrew, I did not stay him. I was thrown, momentarily, into a kind of panic. In a sense, my talk several evenings since with M. Vaignon should have prepared me for this further shock, yet I had still tended then, I think, to discount a good deal of his discourse as crazy ranting – which he had not repeated and, probably, repented. But now the story, borne out in another mouth, had gained fresh substance and solidity. Something – a mortuary breath of evil – had addressed me, subverting reason and defeating sanity. 'Raoul' – if it were he . . . dead eighty years ago. . . . Or what would lead this steady countryman and sober citizen thus to accost me so suspiciously and reprehendingly?

Waiting only until he disappeared across a field, I walked quickly back to the château.

That same evening I got M. Vaignon's consent to my begging Goderich, if he could possibly arrange it, to join me at the earliest opportunity. I had spent six days here, quite uselessly. My boy remained obdurate in avoiding me, keeping out of doors as much as he could and eating his meals I knew not when nor precisely where. This could not go on indefinitely, and he must be removed somehow, but I did not feel confident of my ability to hale him home single-handed, or wish, either, to invoke police assistance, French or British. I worded my letter to Goderich very strongly and, having posted it, was slightly easier in mind.

Otherwise, I was more tortured by anxiety than ever, and my discovery of the lonely grave had had a horrible effect on me. Coupled with the queer manner of the honest fellow who had spoken to me beside it – his doubting, fearful looks and his ambiguous reticence – it left me prey to a complete bewilderment and cold dismay.

Of Denis, meanwhile, as I have just said, I caught only fleeting glimpses. M. Vaignon, who had warned me that he, Denis, would 'try to get it back,' pretended to have interceded with him, but on this I placed no least reliance. I had little real idea of what my boy did with himself all day, of whether he still slept in the same room (though I was assured this was so) or of when he fed, or bathed, or changed his clothes. As to this last point, I had brought with me for him some clean shirts, socks and underwear, which I had handed to Dorlot and were now, I was informed, in use. But, generally, it seemed to me, his condition was one almost of semi-vagabondage, the château being for him not much more than a base or headquarters from which to 'forage' in the countryside.

However, the next morning I did have news of him which, while unreassuring, was somewhat more detailed than previous accounts. Denis, Dorlot remarked, had latterly been spending a good deal of his time in the east wing 'near the tower.' But on my asking what my boy was doing there the man had shrugged. '*Qui sait, Mon-*

sieur? I have seen him reading, or carving wood with his knife. . . .'

'Is he there now?'

'*Non, Monsieur*. It was yesterday and the day before. This morning he has gone out.'

This conversation had been at my *petit déjeuner*, which I always had alone, my host preferring his brought to his bed. After the meal I busied myself in writing a short note to my faithful Jenny, from whom I had heard two days ago. She had reported all well at home, and that she and Clara were hoping, poor things, to welcome us *both* back very soon.

I went out to post my reply to her, struck, as I passed beneath the *porte-cochère*, by the château's latter-day appearance of neglect. It was as if it lay under a spell – as if some blight, of doom and galloping decay, attacked it. Yes – and assailed its inmates too, I thought – one Colonel Walter Habgood not excepted! *I*, to be sure, was only a temporary occupant of the place, a guest, yet I was conscious, whenever I walked abroad, that something of its ill-repute attached to me. With the local peasantry I, too, was in bad odour, the carrier of an aura, an aroma, of the dimly sinister and menacing. And when I had mailed my letter to Goderich yesterday at the little office three kilos up the road to Foant whither I now again was on my way, the postmistress had eyed me balefully, touching her scapular as I was leaving. Go where I might, a species of anxious hostility attended me, expressed in covert stares, in sullen glances, crossings and avoidances. Even the children scattered from my path.

What *was* the truth, I demanded for the hundredth time, about this whole fantastic business? These yokels (*and* M. Vaignon, I suspected) were abjectly superstition-ridden. You might suppose a recent world-war would have knocked such nonsense out of them, but – suddenly, and wryly, I laughed at myself – though it wasn't at all funny. Yes, that was rich! Talk of the pot and kettle . . . ! For *I* was equally in thrall to a grotesque myth with any of the folk I was deriding.

It was exasperating not to know quite what I did believe or disbelieve. Everything and everybody seemed to be conspiring to throw dust in my eyes and keep me ignominiously in the dark. Here was I, Denis's own father, thankful when I could pick up, as just now, a few crumbs of second-hand intelligence about him from a conceited surly menial like Dorlot! More than once, latterly, I had been tempted to question the fellow bluntly, about many things, but hitherto my pride had not allowed me to interrogate the man behind his master's back. As for the master aforesaid, M. Vaignon, since his first outburst, had retired completely into his shell and been as cordially informative as any oyster.

I felt I could endure this mystifying and maddening secretiveness no longer. I must request from someone – anyone – a forthright explanation of the whole enigma and see, at least, what sort of answer was provoked. Accordingly, when I had posted my letter to Jenny, I asked the postmistress to direct me to some person of responsibility – the *maire*, perhaps, or schoolmaster – with whom I could discuss a private matter.

The woman regarded me dirtily enough, replying only after a suspicious pause 'The *maire* is ill,' she said, 'but there is M. Boidilleule the *garde champêtre, qui était de la résistance* and is ill likewise, or M. Tanvy the pharmacien. M. Tanvy,' she added more amiably, 'is very clever, and of a great discretion, having been a quartermaster in the army. . . . Then there is too, of course, Père Puindison, the *curé*. . . .'

Rejecting the belauded M. Tanvy, I decided on the *curé* – an obvious choice which it was strange had not occurred to me before. There was no difficulty in locating him. He had just returned from Mass and welcomed me into his *vicairie* politely.

Somewhat haltingly I outlined as much as necessary of my story, including, particularly, my discovery of the grave. Was, I enquired, the 'Raoul' for whom my boy had this unfortunate infatuation a grandson, possibly, of the deceased?

The *curé*'s face had darkened and at my final question wore a look of, as it were, a scandalised discomfiture. I was quite sure he had known all about me in advance.

'*Franchement, Monsieur*, it is not easy to reply. This is a district *assez superstitieux* and. . . . *Enfin*, the individual whose grave you saw up there at Saint Orvin had no descendants. He was, it would appear, a butler at the château Vaignon, where, actually, he died. But that was eighty years ago, and. . . .'

'Yes, yes,' I said. 'But – but this other fellow, that my boy met. . . . Who is *he* . . . ?'

The good father blinked at me morosely. He was an elderly, florid-visaged man, with eyes that were worldly but, at the moment, troubled and unsubtle.

'*Monsieur*,' he said, reproachfully, 'you come to me, like this, and ask me – what? To confirm and to endorse a doubt that has, beforehand, been implanted in your mind – or maybe to deny it. I can state to you only that the Privache we *know* of died in 1873. The rest is – is merely superstition.'

'And the superstition is – ?'

He shrugged weakly, uncomfortable and disdainfully apologetic under my pressure. '*Evidemment*, the superstition you insist that I enunciate so clearly is that the Privache who died in 1873 and he for whom, you say, your boy has this *engouement* are one and the same . . . *C'est ridicule! Alors* . . . And I have told you, *absolument*, all I can. . . .'

His manner, while still courteous, showed the beginnings of a self-protective frostiness, and again, marvelling, I felt defeated. All these folk, when you tried to tackle them and pin them down upon the subject of this preposterous myth, affected superiorly to scoff at it – yet all of them, in their hearts, were really scared of it!

Thanking the *curé*, I took my dissatisfied and disappointed leave.

I had been at the château just a week – an utterly, completely useless week!

Each day, I had sought every chance of pleading with my boy, so far quite unavailingly. Must I then drag him home a literal captive and so make him hate me worse than ever? Possibly, if need be, but not till I had tried every other, more persuasive measure. Denis was like a wild thing, a wild thing piteously spellbound and enchanted, and it would profit little, I thought, to trap and pinion the poor body if the spirit still eluded me. I wished to snare him – yes – but to snare the whole of him, and lovingly; and bonds and handcuffs seemed an unhappy way of doing this.

Yet if he would not voluntarily come with me there was nothing for it but a degree of force, and it had been with this necessity in closer prospect that I appealed to Goderich, whose sympathetically auxiliary convoy, at the pinch, would certainly be less humiliating than that of a police escort!

In this pass, M. Vaignon was a broken reed, his nerve-racked inanition now, indeed, almost amounting to a kind of passive, undeclared resistance. And why, after exploding as violently as he had about his blessed '*sans-noms*,' had he stopped short there? The *curé* had grudgingly enlightened me to the limit that his scruples or timidity allowed

– but why couldn't M. Vaignon have told me all this, and more, himself?

I walked to the window of my breakfast room and surveyed the autumn fields. From here, they were visible, in brown or sallow squares, stretching irregularly up a saucer's rim to misty hillocks, and in one of them, far off, I fancied, with a start, that I saw Denis. But no, the figure was motionless, and I remembered now that it was only a scarecrow, lingering purposelessly in the stubble.

My letter should reach Goderich today, and, if and when he came, we could hold some sort of council of war. How glad I would be of his refreshing sanity and clearer judgment! My own ideas had become quite chaotic and my affronted reason hurled itself hour by hour against brick walls of contradiction. It was a veritable antinomy. On the one hand, here was the mid-twentieth century, with (even in this backwater) the trains, post, newspaper and radio (should M. Vaignon but elect to buy a set) and an occasional *avion* droning overhead; while, on the other, equally compulsive of assent, there lay – sheer mediaevalism, rank mythology, a weird anachronism of fantastic horror. The two worlds, though interpenetrating, were irreconcilable – and each was true.

I went undecidedly towards my room and then, passing it, along a series of corridors. I had often roamed unchallenged up and down the château's twisting stairs, beneath its faded tapestries and seigneurial banners and across its echoing halls; and now, uneasily while unpremeditatedly enough, my steps trended in the direction of the east wing and its tower.

Nothing in particular rewarded my reconnoitre, if it were one, though in a chamber just below the so-called 'haunted' room I did find a few chips and shavings of the sticks, presumably, that as Dorlot informed me Denis had been whittling. It was not till I had redescended that a speculation springing from my recent conversation with the *curé* crossed my mind. 'Raoul,' père Puindison had stated, had died in the château – and Denis, long ago, as I could now also remember, had said, in speaking of the turret room, that 'someone died there.'

Was the 'someone' Raoul, and was it actually in the tower that he had died? It seemed more than probable.

I spent the rest of the morning and most of the afternoon in desultory 'mooching,' too anxious and distracted, till at least I had Goderich's reply, to settle definitely to anything.

My visit to the east wing and my ensuing conjecture about Raoul had, admittedly, disturbed me, but, beyond that, I seemed dimly conscious of some other cause of a vague apprehension or dissatisfaction. It was something – I had the feeling – that had happened, or that I had briefly noticed, during the course of the day, but which I could not quite lay my finger on – something of which the impact had been oblique and that now tapped irritatingly, with an obscure persistent warning, at my mind. For a time, I tried vainly to recall it, whatever it had been, then gave it up.

I wandered, restively, into the 'library' again and took out the volume of 'Legends,' despite a kind of contemptuous repugnance, to consider, more attentively, what it might have to say.

Presently I found the passage I wanted. It was in a long section entitled, simply, *Auvergne*, and its immediate context was rather mystifying – too occult or too rhapsodical in diction for me to follow clearly. Regretting the inadequacy of my French, I read on, puzzled. '. . . exceptional tenacity of life . . . enabling the said nameless to withdraw vital force . . .' (a line or two here that I could not make head or tail of). '. . . so to rebuild itself around the mammet as around a nucleus or focus and . . .' (again a string of unfamiliar words defeated me). '. . . or other homely object, so be it have the semblance of a man. But woe to all who do adventure thus, and whether child or woman, if the right fixative be not supplied. . . .' And then some sentences of what appeared to be a sort of general description: '. . . their chief weakness being in the wrists and wattles. Yellow above all they joy in, and a certain tint of bluish grey they do defy, wherefore, in extirpating them – . . .'

Disappointed at my stumbling translation, I rested the volume, open, on my knee, and pondered. In a sense, what I *had* managed to translate relieved me, because it seemed such arrant, puerile nonsense. Why yes, I thought, in a delighted welling of, as it were, half-hesitant astonished thankfulness, it *was* all nonsense. Sheer, utter nonsense, and I *could* laugh at it. How had I ever – My fleeting elation ebbed. But Denis – I remembered . . . Yet Denis . . . That was the trouble. 'Nonsense' or no, my boy's plight was actual enough, and –

My host entered – suddenly and brusquely. Owing, ostensibly, to his continued indisposition, we had scarcely encountered for the last several days, and his face now wore a slight frown. '*Bonjour,*' he greeted, peevishly. 'I – I regret to see you so poorly entertained. You will hardly derive much profit, or even amusement I should think, from *that*. . . .' To my amazement he swooped upon the volume and replaced it smartly in the shelves.

Really, M. Vaignon was very trying; and it was now, all in an instant, that, as the result of this comparatively trivial incident, I found myself having an outright, first-class row with him. No doubt, on each side, nerves were frayed to breaking point, and it had needed but this spark to set our tempers in a blaze.

I had stood up. 'You might, *Monsieur*, at least have had the courtesy not to *snatch* from my very knees a book that I was actually reading . . . !'

He glared at me, out of eyes swimming with tears. 'It is my book. It is *my* book,' he repeated childishly, 'and I shall do, as I believe you say, what I bloody well like with it! I am going to bloody-burn it. There *Monsieur*! Can you advance any argument against my bloody-burning my own property, including the entire château, if I see fit? And should anybody still insist on lingering – on *lingering* I say – in this so-charming château of mine *when* I burn it, he will be burnt too, neck and crop, along with it, unless. . . .'

Staggering, he had clapped a hand to his breast. 'Forgive me. . . . I am desolated to have made such an exhibition of myself and caused you to think me like – like a stage-Frenchman, *n'est-ce pas*, but – but certain things in this establishment are not quite as they should be. . . . A large – an infinitely large – bluebottle has got loose in my bedroom and kept me awake all night, and I, too, am as your *sans-noms* – weak in the wrists and wattles . . . !'

Was he going mad? Or shamming mad? *'My' sans-noms!* I was really completely disgusted with him, the more so perhaps because he had somehow succeeded, in this ridiculous fashion, in taking the wind out of my sails.

'This creature of yours, whatever it is,' I was startled to hear myself shouting, 'this precious *sans-nom* of *yours*, I say, that has attacked my boy and that for some reason you'll tell me nothing more about – he died here, didn't he? Up in the tower room, or under it. . . .'

M. Vaignon regarded me, at first uncomprehendingly and then almost as if pityingly. 'My poor friend,' he said slowly. 'My poor friend – all this has been too much for you and – and, ha, ha, you are going crazy. *Mon dieu, c'est le comble, ça!*' He approached nearer, with a curious dancing step and, to my utter dumfounding, snapped a finger and thumb beneath my nose. 'I repeat it, *Monsieur*. I repeat, with inexpressible regret, that you are quite demented!'

I had backed from him, far too bewildered to feel insulted by the taunting words and gesture, and it was at this instant that, as at a previous, somewhat similar, crisis, the tall form of Dorlot filled the doorway.

'*Calmez-vous, mon maître*,' he remonstrated. '*Calmez-vous!* It is this heavy weather that surcharges the nerves, but to yield to your temperament in this manner and with these antics is unseemly. *Calmez-vous!* Thank heaven,' he added in a lower tone, 'it cannot last much longer now.'

M. Vaignon looked at us wildly. 'Forgive me,' he murmured again, 'forgive me. . . .' A strange expression, a sort of leering, still half-impudent despair, flickered over his features as, turning, he let Dorlot lead him unsteadily away.

I stayed motionless where I was a full minute. The whole scene had been incredible, and bedlam had flowered, unashamed, before my eyes.

At length, dazedly, I walked from the house.

Outside, I recovered. That was, my immediate emotional disturbance gradually died down, – but I felt exhausted, as if I had been through a fight or in a mêlée, and my fundamental apprehension and confusion were increased.

It is a nightmare, I thought, a nightmare. That is why everyone appears mad and why you yourself behave like a madman. All at once you will wake up – perhaps when Goderich comes. . . .

The air, as Dorlot had observed, was close and muggy. It was mild, but with a treacherous intimation of tenseness – of I did not quite know what. The fields stretched round me passively – too passively I fancied oddly, as if conspiring, or abandoned, to a gathering sly enchantment. They rolled, in their meek rectangles of ochre, dun and beige, up to unstirring foothills, dreaming a guileful dream. Crossing one of them, I remarked, idly, that the scarecrow I had noticed earlier from the salon window seemed to have altered its position slightly.

M. Vaignon . . . Good heavens! *'Sans-noms'* . . . *! His*, if you please, not mine! I wished him joy of them! *'Sans-noms'!* Ye gods . . . ! Who would invent such bogeys, such farcically loathsome things, unless . . . I raised my eyes to the grey bated sky, and shivered. No, I was not, to word it temperately, much enamoured of this devil's nook, this baleful twelfth- or thirteenth-century pocket of provincial France, where superstitions and obscene mythologies, instead of just remaining quaintly decorative, had the unpleasant trick of springing suddenly alive and driving mad all those who brooded on them overlong. If only . . .

My disjointed ruminations petered out. Once more I raised my eyes, with a faint shudder. All about me, as I walked, the hills, the waiting fields, kept quiet pace with me. I was aware – how shall I put it? – of a bland banking-up, of a demure stealth, a kind of tiptoe ripening of something. . . . My head ached and I had an indescribably oppressive feeling. The château, from the spot where I had now come rather giddily to a halt, was visible, maybe a kilo off, but partially obscured by a dip and by a thin belt of trees. I would get back to it as quickly as I could in case my disagreeable symptoms should increase.

Slowly, I proceeded, conscious, upon my mental palate, of some recrudescent flavour that was dimly nauseous and half-familiar. I had covered perhaps a third of the distance to the château when a dog ran up behind me, whining. It was one of the three or four dogs of the house, an amiable enough little creature, mainly poodle, called Zizi. Denis had been fond of it, and I supposed it still companioned him in his present, gipsyish style of life. But now it appeared distressed or frightened and slunk whimpering and cringing at my heels.

We went on together, skirting a field of stubble. It was the field containing the useless scarecrow, and again, puzzled, I had the impression that the object had moved slightly, in the direction of the château. Hang it! I thought querulously in a sort of mildly annoyed perplexity, this was preposterous, and I must previously have misjudged the confounded thing's position. Zizi, beside me, cowered closer and gave, very low, a series of curious suppressed yelps.

The day had grown overcast and my headache was no better. I had a sense of something brewing, something 'making' – a kind of dumbly guarded watchfulness or wakefulness – in the dull air, the trees, the hilltops and the whelming sky, as if they too were, like myself, alerted and upon some strange and semi-animate *qui-vive*. The dog, while we passed opposite the middle of the field, darted for a moment from me and through the hedge, venting two stiff little barks, of actual terror or of a variety of canine scandal.

Gradually, as we neared the house, my head ached less, yet a conviction of uneasy imminence, a presentiment of swiftly gathering evil, knocked still at my mind's door, and again, more fervently, I longed for Goderich.

I entered the château, and there, on a tray in the hall, lay an answer to my prayer. Yes, said the telegram, he could come, on Tuesday, – that was, in three days' time.

IV

THIS heartening news was confirmed in a letter from him the next morning, explaining that he would have joined me instantly had not his partner been somewhat indisposed and hardly capable, till the promised Tuesday, of shouldering the extra work. Well, it was more than I had had the right to hope that my friend should have been able to arrange to get away at all, and, heaven knew, I blessed him.

During the weekend, however, my feeling of tension increased, and was appreciably heightened, as it happened, by my host's ill-humour. M. Vaignon, after our recent row, had offered me a somewhat grudging apology for his rudeness – but now he was exasperated again upon a different score. While *I* had had, from Goderich, a cheering and reassuring letter, *he* had received, it seemed, a violently upsetting one. The aunt, he told me, with whom *les petits* had been staying had written saying she was compelled to visit Tunisie on business, it might be for several months, and must accordingly send her brother-in-law's children home.

'It is an excuse!' he fumed. '"Business" . . . Pah! They *cannot* come here yet – not yet!'

My sympathy for him, when I remembered the plight of my own boy, was not excessive, and privily I blamed no aunt for getting sick of young Marcel and Augustine, but the matter set my mind running, with a revival of curiosity, on the connection (or in the case of Denis actual relationship) between our respective families, for it was through the sister of this same discredited and disobliging lady that it existed. She had been, before her marriage to M. Vaignon, a Mlle. Drouard, and, by a common ancestor three generations back, a cousin (though I do not think they knew each other) of my wife's.

This train of thought led naturally to a reconsideration of the whole question of M. Vaignon's conduct and attitude throughout; and here I was as far as ever from a satisfactory conclusion. He had blown hot and cold and been, by turns, solicitous and callous, courteous and grossly impolite. He had been contrite enough (if it were that) to break off the 'holiday exchange' arrangement, yet insufficiently honest to warn me, plainly, about Raoul. He had had the grace, later, to wire me twice after Denis had run away to France, but then, when I arrived for the retrieval of my truant, had given me no help. There was no making the man out. . . .

I had been puzzling, alone, upon the Saturday evening, over these and allied problems when I heard a confused noise of angry shouting. The sounds seemed to come from the direction of the stables, suggesting by their volume and persistence that several persons, possibly a dozen or so, were engaged in a violent fracas. But by the time I had gone out to look, just as the hubbub had rather suddenly subsided, the disputants must evidently have stopped their fight, and scattered. Crossing the *basse cour*, however, I saw a man, limping painfully and holding a bloodstained rag to his face. I recognized him as a fellow I had noticed driving one of the wagons that carried hay, or milk and butter from the *laiterie*, and might have asked him what the trouble was had I not at that moment caught, from somewhere within, the shrilly furious tones of M. Vaignon.

As to this incident it was again from Dorlot that I received enlightenment, incomplete though it was. His master (who made no allusion to the matter) having retired immediately after dinner, he, Dorlot, brought me my customary glass of lonely brandy in the library and said: 'That parcel of rascals from Saint Orvin were after Batiste and your boy this afternoon, and nearly had them too . . . !'

'What!' I exclaimed, alarmed. 'After my boy? What for? Is he all right?'

The man replied, coldly, addressing the ceiling, it appeared, rather than me.

'The young *monsieur* is entirely unharmed, since they were unable to catch him, but Batiste – that one, he certainly got a scratch or two. . . .'

'But why – why should they be attacked?'

Dorlot shrugged, spreading his hands. 'People here, *Monsieur*, are superstitious. They are believers in all kinds of nonsense, and possibly the young *monsieur* had been doing something, quite inadvertently, which caused them to suspect him, *sans dire* most wrongfully, of dealing in – in such matters. I cannot tell . . . *Enfin*, the two of them, he and Batiste, were pursued by this band of ignoramuses and ruffians into our very yard, where they found refuge. It is unfortunate,' he added as if meditatively, 'that certain, even, of our own servants, too, should take sides with this rabble. . . . Enough – It is no longer my affair or properly my concern. I leave this place tomorrow. . . .'

I was exceedingly disturbed, not only by Dorlot's story and its implications but also, if to a less degree, by his announcement of departure. It would have been foolish to regard him as an ally, yet he had not been actively hostile and latterly had constituted almost my only source of news concerning Denis.

As to the tale itself – more lay behind it, obviously, than Dorlot would disclose, but of this I could guess at a good deal. Amongst the peasantry Denis would but too naturally be a prime object of suspicion, and it was really a wonder he had evaded molestation (if he had) till now. The man Batiste, surmisably, had been his friend or his associate and fallen, consequently, under the same stigma. . . . Evidently, the business had attained the proportions of a feud, and

M. Vaignon's ranks, within the château, had been split. Dorlot, I fancied, would not lack company upon the train tomorrow. . . .

While I was counting the hours to Goderich's arrival with a fresh sense of urgency I renewed, vainly, my efforts to lessen Denis's hostility. I no longer hoped, now, for a full reconciliation so speedily, but, short of that, I would have liked, before Goderich lent me what help he could, to be at all events on speaking terms with my own child.

Twice I tried to talk with him through his locked door, receiving on the first occasion no reply and on the second the response: 'Oh, go away! I *hate* you!' And twice, also, I got within undignified hailing distance of him in the grounds, only to be humiliated by his almost offhandedly contemptuous flight. Obviously, at any time, I might probably have rallied M. Vaignon's odds and ends of still faithful retainers (a further couple had left with Dorlot in the morning!) to round up my quarry, and then forced him, as my prisoner, to parley – but such trappings or waylayings would have been very much against the grain and, as I saw it then, have done more harm than good.

What, I would wonder, could be his view of the position? How, in his own opinion, was he faring? Pretty evidently he had expected, or at least hoped, to find his odious playmate here – and had not M. Vaignon told me that he, Denis, would do his best to get Raoul back? In that, however, so far as I could judge, he had been disappointed. What had become of the physical 'Raoul' – of the physical 'aspect' of him – I had no idea. Presumably, after my half-throttling of him, he had returned somehow to France, but had not yet (I trusted) reappeared in his old haunts. Upon this point I could have, to be sure, no certainty, but, whoever or whatever the creature was, its headquarters seemed to lie on this side of the Channel, and the next step of minimum precaution was to transport Denis to the other.

Monday – and tomorrow Goderich would be here. Indeed, a letter for him, *aux soins de* M. Vaignon, had rather surprisingly preceded him already, arriving together with one for me from Jenny. The weather was still gloomy, rainless but boding, and again I strolled dejectedly around the nearer fields.

The landscape, as before, was sere and sullen, but its mood, to my imagining, had subtly changed. The sense of stealthy ferment and evil quickening had departed, and the drab acres had an empty look, as if delivered or relieved of something. Loth to accuse myself of being over-fanciful, I stared about me, seeking for anything that might account, more factually, for this impression, but could find nothing. Merely, the scarecrow I had noticed formerly had gone, having been removed and set up for whatever none too obvious reason, as I subsequently discovered, in another field considerably closer to the house.

I wandered slowly back to the château. Help was at last at hand – for Goderich should be here tomorrow evening – yet my heart was curiously unlightened. The countryside, louring and secret, with that discharged and voided aspect of an ominous fulfillment, seemed to wear a mien of hidden ridicule, of some kind of deceptive somnolence and inward mockery, as though it were laughing at me up its sleeve. Nonsense! I tried to think. What utter nonsense . . . ! With a derisive apt theatricality a trio of stage-property bats, encouraged by the dusk, skimmed past me as I turned by the corner of a barn.

And then, suddenly, I had a shock.

'Hello, Daddy . . . ,' said Denis.

He was there, in front of me, shyly smiling and addressing me in this form he had discarded, for some years, as 'babyish.' His clothes were stained and torn and his cheeks wan under their grime. I did not believe he had washed properly for days.

But it was far less his ragamuffin air that horrified me than his manner. It was flat and almost bored, yet confident; casual and unconstrained in some utterly wrong way, as though he were so tired out with whatever he had been up to that he had forgotten, even, what it was. How could he, else, have carried it off with this weary, this to me actually hideous, aplomb? He stood, gazing at me in a sort of forlorn and rather vacant friendliness, as if nothing had happened, as if he were completely unconscious of my misery, or his own.

'Come in,' I think I said to him. 'And – and talk things over, shall we . . . ?'

'Yes . . . ,' he replied absently. 'All right. I'm hungry too.' He paused, then added, reconsideringly and as a careful qualification, 'That is, you know, not really *very*. . . .'

We had begun to walk on, from the barn, and the fading light shone, briefly, on his face, discovering there a look that sickened me but is not easy to describe. It was at once wily and exhausted, an expression so to speak of a supreme irrelevance or imperviousness to the situation, of a precocious unconcern and hard frivolity or falsity – a falsity all the worse for being undeliberate and still childish. My gorge rose as at something odious. Rage filled me and, to my dismay, I found my fist clenched to strike him. It was with the greatest effort that I controlled the impulse.

'Denis . . . ,' I heard myself saying. '*Denis . . . !*' My anger had turned suddenly to yearning and I had him, unresisting, in my arms. He was light as a feather, limply yielding, and weighing nothing, almost nothing. I felt, while I strained him to me, as if he were liable at any instant to melt away from my embrace into thin air.

At the château, when we entered, M. Vaignon had

just come into the hall, gaping at us as though quite confounded.

I do not really know how the next few hours passed, what words were said or what was done in them. I do know and remember that they were not happy or triumphant hours – alas, far from that. A deep emotional conviction of impending sorrow or calamity persisted and I could not banish it. Superficially, it was to the good that the pursuits, the trappings and lassoings I had envisaged were dispensed with – yet what had I instead? *Not* Denis. That was the trouble. It was only the curious shell of him I had. He was a wanling, almost a changeling – something that most horribly denied each trait and feature of the Denis I recalled, and of which the contemplation could but be agonizing.

None the less, as I say, this unexpected turn of events was a practical simplification. Presumably, Denis would 'come quietly' and not have to be dragged home a prisoner. Goderich, when he arrived, would have nothing to do but go back with us again. And then . . . ?

'Are you tired?' I believe I asked once, 'after all the – the camping-out . . . ?'

He regarded me queerly, head cocked, with the suspicious, quasi-intelligent incomprehension, the notion visited me dreadfully, of a parrot. 'A – a little. Yes, a little. . . .'

That was all; but the manner if not the matter of the reply had remained vaguely hostile – and violently unsatisfactory. His tone held a deplorable sort of cunning, or of fancied cunning – as if, despite his sudden yielding, he still had an ace hidden somewhere in the pack, or thought he had.

What had prompted his surrender? Had he merely wearied of roughing it and craved the ordinary home comforts he had missed, now, for three weeks? Had his designs, whatever was their nature, been frustrated, or miscarried, so that at last he had had to give them up? Or had he, possibly, decided that my reinforcement by Goderich (of whose coming, apart from servants' gossip, he could have got wind in any case from the letter in the hall) would be too much for him and that he might as well cave in to me right away?

I must wait to find out all that, for the time was not propitious yet, I felt, for direct catechisings. Fortunately, perhaps, for that evening at any rate this question did not arise, as Denis professed himself so drowsy that, as soon as he had had his tea, and then a bath, he went to bed.

Of M. Vaignon, save for his startled apparition in the hall, I had seen nothing since lunch. I dined alone and, after a couple of pipes in the *petit salon*, was glad to get up to my room.

Denis and I, I reflected, had forgotten, or at least – perhaps on both sides semi-deliberately – omitted, to say goodnight to each other. I wondered whether he were yet awake, or (if his sleep were half as troubled as I feared likely in his father's case) what dreams would visit him.

Next day, I was in two minds about taking Denis with me to the station to meet Goderich, deciding finally against it. I did not think he would slip off again, and if he did it would only prove his capitulation no real capitulation after all. As to that, indeed, I still felt something disquietingly planned or spurious in it; but my misgivings did not include, now, any apprehensions of his renewed and literal bolting.

Nothing much had happened during the morning. M. Vaignon, encountering me just before lunch, congratulated me, with a deathly simper, on my improved *entente* with Denis and made no difficulties over lending me the car, which I was mightily relieved he did not propose to drive, this time, himself. Goderich would stay one night at the château, and tomorrow the three of us would return to England.

I pictured my friend's surprise when he learned of the fresh development. In a sense he would have had his journey for nothing, but I didn't think he would mind that. A wire yesterday evening might just have caught and stopped him, – but, actually, Denis's unexpected 'surrender' had put everything else out of my head, and I was selfishly glad, now, that it had.

At the station, I had still ten minutes to wait, and outside the yard entrance to the baggage-office I noticed a wagon drawn up, and a long box being unloaded from it and then carried in to the clerk. The wagon I could recognize as from the château, and the fellow awkwardly shouldering the box was, I was pretty sure, that same 'Batiste' I had seen limping, with the bloodstained kerchief to his face, in the *basse cour* two days ago. As he climbed again into his seat, the *chef de gare* himself came out to confer for a few moments with him in an undertone.

But here at last was Goderich's train. It had scarcely clanked puffing to a standstill before he leaped out and clasped my hand in his.

'Well,' he was saying, 'it's rather like one's toothache's fleeing on the dentist's doorstep. If I hadn't "come for nothing," as you are so kind as to suggest, you and your young jackanapes would probably still be at logger-heads.'

We were approaching the château, and I wondered. Goderich's hearty vigour, his very tone of cheerful lightness, was a gust of health and hope from another world – and yet, I doubted, and was even, somehow, shocked.

'If we're *not* still at loggerheads, as it is,' I remember answering. 'You'll see for yourself presently.'

We drove under the *porte-cochère*, and alighted. M. Vaignon was there to greet us, all politeness. A small, dim figure hung back, hugging the shadows.

'Hello, scallywag!' called Goderich. 'Hi, come out of that!'

Denis moved forwards undecidedly. His face, again, horrified me by its hollow wanness.

''M . . . ,' Goderich commented. 'Not altogether a walking advertisement of anything, I must say. That's the deserts of being A. W. O. L. . . . Nineteen days adrift, eh? But we won't clap him in the glass-house this time, sergeant-major. . . .'

Once more, I gave a mental gasp. I did not know whether to admire or be scared out of my wits by Goderich's breeziness. Wasn't it, I misdoubted, a trifle overdone? It jolted me, I think, not so much through a fear of its effect on Denis as by appearing almost *too* temerarious a defiance of the evil gods.

But Denis did not seem to mind this 'joshing.' He even smiled faintly, as Goderich persevered with his hardy badinage, and ate, under the friendly bombardment, a reasonably good tea.

None the less, I could divine, beneath his fun-poking, that Goderich was concerned. When Denis had gone off, 'to see the horses fed' he said, with Zizi, my friend's expression became grave.

'What do you make of this, Habgood?' he surprised me by enquiring.

'*I* . . . ? Why, I – I want *you* to tell *me*!'

'Of course. But first I'd be interested in your opinions, so far as you have any. Do you, for instance, really – .' He broke off: 'Wait a bit. Are we likely to be disturbed here? Our perfect host isn't liable to butt in, is he?'

'I shouldn't think so. He's completely haywire these days, and we probably won't see him again this evening.'

'Suits me. . . . And if – .'

But at this moment, to falsify my prophecy, M. Vaignon *did* 'butt in,' insisting upon 'entertaining' us, with the most oddly vapid small talk, until and throughout dinner; and it was only when he had at length proffered his excuses and retired that I and Goderich could continue our discussion. Denis himself, as on the previous night, had gone early to his bed.

'Well,' Goderich resumed, 'what *is* your feeling, about the whole thing, now? For example – and putting a conceivable crackbrained 'impersonation' out of it, as I think we may – do you actually believe that the pernicious loon we both knew down in Hampshire is the same Privache whose grave, you've said, you saw near here last week?'

'It – it certainly *sounds* nonsense,' I replied.

' "Nonsense" – yes, naturally it does. But even nonsense can be dynamic. In its proper realm, where its writ runs and it holds sway, it *isn't* nonsense. And it can, often, effectually intrude into a sphere beyond its own. It has become at least *mentally* real for Denis, and also, up to a point, for you. I just wanted to know how real.'

'I tell you, I don't know. It simply doesn't add up.'

'All right. It doesn't. If it *did*, for instance, this damned sallydore could eventually be traced, and be run-in for something. But for what, exactly? In what terms could you prefer a charge? I'd hate to see you trying! The notion would be quite absurd – which just shows you that it *can't* "add up" for us in any ordinary way. But the next obvious practical step anyhow is to get your boy as clear of it all as we can and pray that later he'll – well, respond to treatment.'

'But what do *you* think, honestly? Is . . . ?' I faltered.

'I know what you're going to ask. Well, *is* it? Or, again,

is it? How can *I* tell? It was *there*, that precious gaby was, and it appeared to be more or less passably a man – and, for some revolting reason, it wore mittens. Also, it had an arm which acted up pretty unorthodoxly. . . . What I *don't* see is how a mere throttling, a semi-throttling, could have snuffed it out and kiboshed it, at all events temporarily, as it seems to have done. . . . No doubt, that rubbed in the fact that it wasn't too popular, and would be a deterrent to some extent, but. . . .'

Goderich, too, hesitated; then went on: 'I don't fancy we can get much forrarder along those lines. It's easy enough to say the whole thing's farcical – and if you could *feel* that as well as say it, it would be fine. What about the 'poltergeist' noises? Do they still go on?'

'I was told so. I've not heard them here myself.'

'And the "haunted" room, where you're persuaded the original fee-faw-fum demised. How does that come into it? Did our host admit definitely that Privache No. 1 *had* died there?'

' "Definitely" . . . ! No indeed. He's never said anything definite or straightforward. When I did as it were challenge him to deny that the – the first Privache had died where I felt he had, he just behaved quite weirdly, was abominably rude, and accused *me* of going mad. . . .'

For some while longer our talk continued without leading us to any more concrete conclusion than we had reached already – that our sole hope for Denis lay in getting him away immediately and that, when this was done, it would be only in the nick of time.

We had thought, Goderich and I, that we were bringing Denis home, and that morning we treated our precious freight as if no precaution for its safety could be excessive. Denis was, actually and in literal truth, so worn and wasted that such an attitude would have been natural in any case, and I think we both felt that, unless the greatest care were exercised, he might as it were collapse in our hands or be blown away by a puff. His eyes were lustreless and his skin dry, and his manner held some ingredient I could not define, at once apathetic and expectant, or perhaps apprehensive.

The day had broken cloudily after, for me, a restless night. I had had dreams, but could not recall them clearly. Mostly, they had been of absurdities – of M. Vaignon addressing a meeting of puppets in the library, of Dorlot roller-skating somewhere overhead, and even of the ridiculous scarecrow, shifting from field to field in a continued march towards the house – but their persisting savour was oppressive, and I had woken from them with nerves jangled.

Our train was to leave Foant at about ten-thirty, and we had risen, we realised, rather unnecessarily early. Denis, glancing at us distraitly from under lowered brows, ate an extremely sketchy breakfast. Once, he appeared lost in a kind of reverie, and then, arousing from it with a start, upset his chocolate bowl. The slight mishap caused him to open his mouth, aghastly, in an unuttered scream.

This time, we wouldn't need our host's car. I had arranged, yesterday, for a taxi to come out for us from Foant, and now I prayed it might be punctual. Our luggage was stacked in the hall; I had tipped the servants, and M. Vaignon, dressing-gowned, had made a grisly mountebank descent to say goodbye. Bowing, and stiffly shaking hands, he muttered something else that sounded like: '. . . if it will let you. . . .'

At last the three of us drove off. For a while, my spirits lightened and I breathed more freely.

'Are you all right?' I asked Denis.

'Oh yes. . . .'

He was next me and facing Goderich, gazing dreamily – or raptly – out of the window. His expression was remote, as though he were attending to something we could not see, or not appreciate. His hair, I noticed, had grown long and wanted cutting.

Suddenly, from under his seat, issued a low bark. Zizi! How he had managed it I did not know, but the little creature must have leaped in after Denis, and we should now have to ask the station-master to restore him to his owner.

This, on alighting from the taxi, we did, and presently the train drew in. Denis, for a second or two as Goderich and I were about to board it, was not to be found, and my heart froze. But next moment he came scurrying from the direction of the *consigne* and clambered in with us just in time.

I was so thankful at retrieving him! A passion of yearning sympathy for my poor darling rose in me, and I pressed his arm. The train gathered speed and I remember sighing in relief and thinking that every mile now was a mile further towards his safety. Actually, I had hardly expected or quite dared to hope we *would* ever do it – ever get away. I had feared, all the while, that something – though I couldn't guess how or what – would happen or put out a hand to halt us or detain us – some sort of accident or hitch – and. . . .

But my satisfaction ebbed, and died. Denis's manner suddenly alarmed me. He was distressed, I could not tell why. 'The – the scare – .' He seemed to be trying, unsuccessfully, to say something; then, changing to French, at length got out: '. . . *l'épouvantail, c'est dans*. . . .' He paused, and added, with an urgency I could not understand, the one word: 'Zizi. . . .'

Sure enough, to my annoyed confusion, the dog was there, and with us still, whether or not with Denis's abetting I did not know. But it was not the dog's presence I was bothered over: it was the curious looks and bearing of my boy.

Another train, which must be an express, was overtaking us, coming up rapidly upon a parallel track. Our own train, as if inspired to a race, increased its speed, and the express gained on us less swiftly. Zizi had burst in upon us, at first delightedly, from the corridor, wagging his tail, but now appeared strangely subdued. With a short bark of half-hearted challenge he slunk cowering under the seat, by Denis.

'What *is* it, Denis? What's the matter?' I implored.

Goderich had pulled out a brandy flask and held it to Denis's lips. They moved slowly and bewilderedly. '*L'épouvantail*. . . . The – the scarecrow . . . *c'est*. . . .'

Suddenly he broke from us, moaning, and dashed into the corridor. Both I and Goderich had grabbed at him, ineffectually. The dog, as though torn between its fear and a kind of loyalty, had emerged from under the seat and stood whimpering in the doorway.

Thrusting it aside with my boot, I followed Denis. The express was quickly overhauling us. I could just see, at the moment, the front of its locomotive showing level with the corridor's end, then creeping foot by foot along our windows.

'Denis, Denis!' I repeated. 'What *is* it? What are you *doing*?'

He was hunched oddly, staring out at the other train with a quite indescribable look of terror on his face. His eyes were round with fright and his body was pressed desperately against the corridor's inner wall as if, despite his fascinated interest, he were trying to get as far from the pursuing coaches as he could.

What followed has an outré horror and grotesqueness which puts such a strain on ordinary credence that even I who witnessed it still find it hard if not impossible at times to reconcile with, or accept as, 'literal' truth. I cannot, in any way, explain it, but I believe, now, that something, then, went hideously wrong – went wrong from Denis's and Raoul's point of view, I mean – and that whatever sort of ghastly schemes and machinations may have been afoot were, at the last moment, bungled. What I did see, or what at all events I seemed to see, was the result, I feel, of some bizarre and odious miscarriage. . . .

I had caught Denis's arm, and shook it, but he paid no attention to me. Two men, on the farther side of him, stuck curious heads out of their compartment, and gaped foolishly at us. Behind me, squeezed up in the narrow passage, Goderich was shouting over my shoulder, above the uproar of the trains: 'Come on, young man, snap out of it! Come back!' His voice was cool, but he added, in my ear: 'For heaven's sake get hold of him somehow!'

Denis had wedged himself against the jamb of a half-open door, and it was now, as I was struggling, in the cramped space, to wrest him from it, that our own pace abruptly slackened, so that the express began to flash by our windows at a rush. I learned later that it was then that Goderich had pulled the communication cord. Meanwhile I still could not drag Denis free. I was aware that he was in some awful danger but tugged at him in vain. As in a nightmare, I strained till the sweat stood on my forehead, praying that the dream would break.

It never did, or has. For an instant I had looked out of the window. The guard's van of the express was just passing us. Something, a long box like a coffin, cocked lewdly up and protruded slowly from it, flew out of it towards us, and crashed against us. The corridor was littered with shivered glass.

The train had stopped with a violent jolt. People were running along the track, and already I caught, from somewhere, amazed exclamations: '*Un épouvantail* . . . ! It was, in that box there, solely a scarecrow . . . !'

I turned again to Denis, thinking I heard his call.

'Zizi . . . ,' I fancied he had said. But what had happened to the dog I did not, then or later, know or care.

My boy's face was seamed and wizened as that of an old man, and the starkest terror was graven on it. His body now was quite limp in my hands.

Goderich and I carried him back to the compartment and laid him on a seat, and it was then I saw that, before his last cry, his hair, which had changed to elf-locks, had gone white.

RECENT AND FORTHCOMING TITLES FROM VALANCOURT BOOKS

Michael Arlen	Hell! said the Duchess
R. C. Ashby	He Arrived at Dusk
Frank Baker	The Birds
H. E. Bates	Fair Stood the Wind for France
Walter Baxter	Look Down in Mercy
Charles Beaumont	The Hunger and Other Stories
	The Intruder
	A Touch of the Creature
David Benedictus	The Fourth of June
Paul Binding	Harmonica's Bridegroom
Charles Birkin	The Smell of Evil
John Blackburn	A Scent of New-Mown Hay
	Broken Boy
	Blue Octavo
	A Ring of Roses
	Children of the Night
	The Flame and the Wind
	Nothing but the Night
	Bury Him Darkly
	The Household Traitors
	Our Lady of Pain
	Devil Daddy
	The Face of the Lion
	The Cyclops Goblet
	A Beastly Business
	The Bad Penny
Thomas Blackburn	A Clip of Steel
	The Feast of the Wolf
Michael Blumlein	The Brains of Rats
John Braine	Room at the Top
	The Vodi
	Life at the Top
Jack Cady	The Well
Michael Campbell	Lord Dismiss Us
David Case	Among the Wolves
	Fengriffen
R. Chetwynd-Hayes	The Monster Club
	Looking for Something to Suck
Isabel Colegate	The Blackmailer

Basil Copper	The Great White Space
	Necropolis
	The House of the Wolf
Hunter Davies	Body Charge
Jennifer Dawson	The Ha-Ha
Frank De Felitta	The Entity
	Golgotha Falls
Lord Dunsany	The Curse of the Wise Woman
A. E. Ellis	The Rack
Barry England	Figures in a Landscape
Ronald Fraser	Flower Phantoms
Michael Frayn	The Tin Men
	The Russian Interpreter
	Towards the End of the Morning
	A Very Private Life
	Sweet Dreams
Gillian Freeman	The Liberty Man
	The Leather Boys
	The Leader
Rodney Garland	The Heart in Exile
Stephen Gilbert	The Landslide
	Bombardier
	Monkeyface
	The Burnaby Experiments
	Ratman's Notebooks
Martyn Goff	The Plaster Fabric
	The Youngest Director
	Indecent Assault
F. L. Green	Odd Man Out
Stephen Gregory	The Cormorant
	The Woodwitch
	The Blood of Angels
Alex Hamilton	Beam of Malice
Thomas Hinde	The Day the Call Came
Claude Houghton	Neighbours
	I Am Jonathan Scrivener
	This Was Ivor Trent
Fred Hoyle	The Black Cloud
Alan Judd	The Devil's Own Work
James Kennaway	The Mind Benders
	The Cost of Living Like This
Cyril Kersh	The Aggravations of Minnie Ashe

Gerald Kersh	Fowlers End
	Nightshade and Damnations
	Clock Without Hands
	Neither Man Nor Dog
	The Great Wash
	On an Odd Note
Francis King	To the Dark Tower
	Never Again
	An Air That Kills
	The Dividing Stream
	The Dark Glasses
	The Man on the Rock
C.H.B. Kitchin	The Sensitive One
	Birthday Party
	Ten Pollitt Place
	The Book of Life
	A Short Walk in Williams Park
Hilda Lewis	The Witch and the Priest
John Lodwick	Brother Death
Robert Marasco	Burnt Offerings
Gabriel Marlowe	I Am Your Brother
Kenneth Martin	Aubade
	Waiting for the Sky to Fall
Robin Maugham	Behind the Mirror
Michael McDowell	The Amulet
	Cold Moon Over Babylon
	The Elementals
Michael Nelson	Knock or Ring
	A Room in Chelsea Square
Beverley Nichols	Crazy Pavements
Arch Oboler	House on Fire
Oliver Onions	The Hand of Kornelius Voyt
Dennis Parry	The Survivor
	Sea of Glass
Christopher Priest	The Affirmation
J.B. Priestley	Benighted
	The Doomsday Men
	The Other Place
	The Magicians
	Saturn Over the Water
	The Shapes of Sleep
	The Thirty-First of June
	Salt Is Leaving

Peter Prince	Play Things
Piers Paul Read	Monk Dawson
Forrest Reid	The Garden God
	Following Darkness
	The Spring Song
	Brian Westby
	Uncle Stephen
	The Retreat
	Young Tom
	Denis Bracknel
Nevil Shute	Landfall
	An Old Captivity
Andrew Sinclair	The Raker
	Gog
	The Facts in the Case of E. A. Poe
Colin Spencer	Panic
David Storey	Radcliffe
	Pasmore
	Saville
Michael Talbot	The Delicate Dependency
	The Bog
	Night Things
Bernard Taylor	The Godsend
	Sweetheart, Sweetheart
	The Moorstone Sickness
Russell Thorndike	The Slype
	The Master of the Macabre
John Trevena	Sleeping Waters
John Wain	Hurry on Down
	The Smaller Sky
	A Winter in the Hills
Hugh Walpole	The Killer and the Slain
Robert Westall	Antique Dust
Keith Waterhouse	There is a Happy Land
	Billy Liar
	Jubb
	Billy Liar on the Moon
Colin Wilson	Ritual in the Dark
	Man Without a Shadow
	The World of Violence
	Necessary Doubt
	The Glass Cage
	The Philosopher's Stone
	The God of the Labyrinth

WHAT CRITICS ARE SAYING ABOUT VALANCOURT BOOKS

'Valancourt are doing a magnificent job in making these books not only available but – in many cases – known at all . . . these reprints are well chosen and well designed (often using the original dust jackets), and have excellent introductions.'

Times Literary Supplement (London)

'Valancourt Books champions neglected but important works of fantastic, occult, decadent and gay literature. The press's Web site not only lists scores of titles but also explains why these often obscure books are still worth reading. . . . So if you're a real reader, one who looks beyond the bestseller list and the touted books of the moment, Valancourt's publications may be just what you're searching for.'

MICHAEL DIRDA, *Washington Post*

'Valancourt Books are fast becoming my favourite publisher. They have made it their business, with considerable taste and integrity, to put back into print a considerable amount of work which has been in serious need of republication. If you ever felt there were gaps in your reading experience or are simply frustrated that you can't find enough good, substantial fiction in the shops or even online, then this is the publisher for you.'

MICHAEL MOORCOCK

'The best resurrectionists since Burke and Hare!'

ANDREW SINCLAIR